Loose Ends

Jeff Erno

Loose Ends

Jeff Erno

Chapter One

Holding the stuffed bear in front of his face, Ivan stepped into the hospital room. He bobbed it up and down, then back and forth, and with a high-pitched Pooh-like voice addressed his patient. "I heard someone's having an operation today!"

"Me! I am!" The four-year old pushed himself up, then leaned forward with outstretched arms to reach for the bear. "I know it's you, Ivan."

"It's me *and* Pooh. And you know what? I talked to the doctor, and she said Pooh can go with you when you go in for your operation."

Jaydin scowled. "Bears can't go in the operating room, can they?" He glanced over to his mother who stood on the opposite side of the bed. She slipped her hand onto the little guy's shoulder.

"Well, honey, they're going to do the operation when you're sleeping. Pooh can stay with you till you fall asleep, and he'll be with you again when you wake up."

"I want him to stay with me the whole time."

"Don't you worry," Ivan assured him. "Pooh will be right there."

"And Daddy!"

Ivan looked up to briefly establish eye contact with Jaydin's mom. "Mommy and Daddy will be here. They'll be waiting for you when you wake up. It's gonna be so quick and easy. You'll close your eyes one second, and the next you'll open them and it will be all over with. And Mommy and Daddy will be there with you."

"Daddy's not here though." Jaydin twisted his face, obviously fighting the urge to cry. He blinked and looked up with his big brown eyes at Ivan. "Do you know where my Daddy is?"

"He's on his way, honey." His mother spoke soothingly, but from the expression on her face, she was as annoyed by her ex-husband's absence as Ivan.

Ivan had been a nurse for four years, the entirety of which he'd worked at St. Joseph's in the pediatric ward. He'd seen hundreds of little angels come into the unit, some for minor operations and many for more serious, life-threatening procedures. Jaydin needed a tonsillectomy, which might not seem a big deal to the boy's father, but if Ivan were the little guy's dad, he'd have been camped out bedside until it was time to take him home. Ivan didn't understand parents like Jaydin's father. Obviously, the little boy idolized his daddy, but the man couldn't be bothered to make it to the hospital in time for his son's surgery.

Ivan walked over to the side of the bed and held out his hand, stroking his fingers across Jaydin's soft curly hair. "Remember the cool Star Wars Band Aid you got when you first came to the hospital?"

"The Storm Trooper?"

"Yup. You want another one like that?"

Jaydin looked up at him, wide-eyed, smiling. "I want Kylo Ren!"

"Kylo Ren? He's a bad guy, isn't he?"

"So's the Storm Troopers. Well, wait. Not all of 'em. Not Finn."

"Hmm." Ivan reached into his pocket and pulled out an assortment of animated bandages. "Let's see. I've got Rey, and here's R2D2, and another storm trooper. I don't have any Kylo."

Jaydin's bottom lip protruded, but only for a second, then he leaned forward to examine the bandages. "I want R2D2." He smiled, arching his eyebrows in the cutest expression Ivan had ever seen, then suddenly grew serious. "Wait! Why do

I get a Band Aid? I don't have a owie." Panicked, he looked up at his mother with pleading eyes. "I don't want a ivy! Mom…" His face began to crinkle into an expression of anguished terror just as Ivan spun around in response to footsteps he heard from behind.

"Hey big guy!" A tall, dark, and handsome white dude stood in the door holding a stuffed Winnie the Pooh bear, about twice the size of the one Ivan had just delivered.

"Daddy! I don't want a ivy!"

So *this* was Jaydin's father? Ivan had assumed the boy's dad was African American like his mother, but this explained Jaydin's lighter skin tone and softer curls.

"Where have you been?" Jaydin's mom barely concealed her irritation of her ex-husband's tardiness. Glaring at him, she crossed her arms over her chest.

"Remember what we talked about, Jay Jay?" The man ignored his ex-wife and moved closer to the bed, holding out his Pooh bear. "We gotta be brave sometimes, even if it means doing things we don't want to do."

"But Daddy! It's like a shot."

Jaydin had been in and out of the hospital quite a bit in his young life, battling numerous throat and ear infections. He also suffered from chronic bronchial asthma, and Jaydin had been hospitalized a couple of times after having attacks. As young as he was, he knew all about hospital procedures, including the dreaded I.V.

Though Ivan had been Jaydin's nurse previously, he'd never met the boy's father. What Ivan did know, however, was that the little boy idolized the man. He was some sort of cop from what Ivan had gathered. Jaydin had repeatedly bragged about how his daddy's job was to catch the bad guys.

"It's just a little teenie, tiny poke, though." Tall, dark, and handsome lowered himself to sit on the edge of the mattress.

"And it's so they can give you medicine when you're having your operation. Right?" He looked up at Ivan for confirmation.

"That's right." Ivan forced a smile, a wave of annoyance sweeping over him. Where was this man the last two hours as his son lay fretting and panicking that his daddy wasn't even going to show up for his operation? And now here he was at last sweeping in to act like the big, badass hero.

Ivan moved to the other side of the bed, stepping around Jaydin's mother as Mr. Macho Police Detective remained next to his son holding the little boy's hand. Ivan ever so gently took hold of Jaydin's other wrist, examining the arm carefully as he sought the best location for insertion of the I.V. needle. Jaydin's father continued to talk to the boy, promising him ice cream and Jell-O with lots of whipped cream after his operation.

As Jaydin engaged with his daddy, completely distracted from what Ivan was doing with his arm, Ivan expertly planted the I.V. Jaydin looked over, only slightly startled by the needle prick, but his daddy gently placed his fingers beneath the boy's chin and guided his gaze back in the other direction, casually acting as if nothing was happening.

Quickly Ivan peeled open the bandage wrapper and secured the R2D2 unit over the taped I.V. port. "There ya go, little man. Good to go. You got your R2 and two Pooh bears."

"And my daddy!"

Jaydin's mom slid next to her son as Ivan gathered up his supplies. "And Mommy," Jaydin added. "Together…like it used to be."

The boy's parents glanced at each other, then each turned to their son, smiling. "No matter what," Jaydin's dad said, "we'll both always be here for our little guy."

"I'm not little no more, Daddy."

"No you're not," his mother said. "You're growing up so fast."

"I'm almost gonna be five, and you promised I can have a party, right?"

"Right." Jaydin's father nodded. "With a Star Wars cake."

"Kylo Ren. I want a Kylo Ren cake!"

~ ~ ~ ~ ~

Every inch of Tucker Brown's six-foot-seven frame tensed with guilt as he sat hunched over in the waiting room chair. He rested his elbows on his knees with his head bowed as his ex-wife read him the riot act.

"Maybe you don't think a minor surgery like this is a big deal. Maybe you consider it routine, but it's not routine to that little boy, that little man who idolizes the ground you walk on, Tuck. He's been fretting since the moment he woke up that his daddy wasn't there yet."

Tucker sighed, shaking his head. "I know. You're right. I should've been here earlier, and I don't think surgery of *any* kind is routine on my...I mean... on *our* son." He looked over to her. "I shouldn't have left."

"What do you mean, you shouldn't have left?"

"Here. I shouldn't have left earlier. I got here at five o'clock this morning. Like an idiot, I brought donuts, Jaydin's favorites, then remembered he couldn't eat anything." Her expression softened, and the corners of her mouth twitched almost unnoticeably. "Then I got a call from work. Which..." He sighed again, more dramatically. "Which I shouldn't have even answered. There's been a fire not far from here, and a woman was killed. I thought I could make it to the scene and check in with Viviano. He'll be assisting with the case. The whole thing was a clusterfuck."

"A woman was killed?" Janelle's words, steeped in empathy, pierced Tucker's heart. She didn't even know the victim, and yet was concerned. It was no wonder he loved her so much. Christ, he always had. They'd been best friends since high school, and she was the only woman he'd ever even thought of marrying. "Tuck, I'm sorry." She slid over to the seat beside him and pressed her fingertips against his arm. "You okay?"

He nodded. "I'm fine. By the time I got there, it was already too late. She was already gone. Her dog too. She was only in her mid-forties."

"But there was foul play?" Janelle knew how it worked. She knew Tucker handled homicides, and he wouldn't have been called to a fire unless there was some evidence it hadn't necessarily been accidental.

"Too early to know anything for sure, but it looks like the fire had been set."

At the moment, Tucker wasn't concerned about the fire. As tragic as the woman's death might be, it wasn't Tucker's primary concern. Jaydin was the only one that mattered right now. In his four short years of life, the little guy had been a trooper. He'd already endured so much, in and out of the hospital so many times. Hopefully the removal of his tonsils would make a difference, but Tucker feared it wouldn't end here. The doctor had already suggested he might have to undergo another surgery to have tubes placed in his ears.

When it came to his own life, Tucker hadn't always made the wisest decisions, but he'd never regret marrying Janelle. Their union had produced the best thing that had ever happened to Tucker. Jaydin was everything to him, and it killed Tucker to see his son suffering. Every kid deserved a happy, healthy childhood, and Jaydin was not just any kid. He was so bright for his age, so understanding beyond his years. And he had such a pure, innocent heart.

Tucker and Janelle shared joint custody. They alternated weekends. Every week, Tucker would have Jaydin either the weekend plus two week days or three weekdays. They divided up the holidays, to keep things fair. But the official schedule didn't really matter. He and Janelle had a very amicable relationship, and they both were committed to doing what was best for their son. They never argued or spoke ill of each other. In fact, they had become even closer friends after the divorce.

Thinking back on what they'd been through in their relationship, Tucker counted his blessings.

"Goddammit, Janelle, will you give it a rest? I don't even know what you're asking. I don't know what you fucking expect from me!"

Tucker ran a hand through his close-cropped hair and turned to stare out the window. The gray sky and steady drizzle of rain provided a befitting backdrop to his melancholy mood. His whole world was crumbling beneath his feet, but he barely felt anything. At this point, his emotions had numbed.

"You weren't at Extasy for a three-hour stakeout, Tucker." She referred to the gay nightclub every man, woman, and child, straight or gay, knew about. Fulton County wasn't exactly a thriving, progressive metropolis. Extasy's reputation as the one-and-only social outlet for LGBT people was solidly established. "And the porn sites? What about them? And... and Tucker." Her voice began to crack. "When was the last time we even made love?"

He spun around to face her, praying his body wasn't visibly trembling as badly as his insides. Was this even happening? This could only be a bad dream, an unthinkable nightmare. "Janelle..." He closed his eyes, then reopened them to stare into hers which were now brimming with tears. Moving closer, he reached out to her, but she quickly pulled back. "I've never cheated," he whispered.

"Only in your heart." Her voice softened to a whisper.

"I love you. Dammit, baby. You know I do. And I love Jaydin...with all my heart."

"But I'm not enough." She stepped over to the bureau and pulled open the drawer where she stashed a pack of cigarettes. They'd both quit smoking before Jaydin was born, but she sneaked one every *now and then. Snatching the pack of Newports and a lighter, she breezed past Tucker and slung open the sliding glass window. Tucker followed her outside as she torched her cigarette then inhaled deeply. He stood beside her watching the stream of exhale smoke, tempted briefly to fire up one of his own. They stood together beneath the overhang as the rain continued its drizzle.*

"I'm sorry." He didn't have the fortitude to continue lying. The lies, especially those he told himself, were exhausting. He couldn't do it anymore. He couldn't continue his charade. "I haven't been with anyone since we started dating. I've thought about it. I've been tempted. But I could never go through with it. I knew I'd never be able to live with myself."

She stared at him for a moment, her eyes boring a hole into his soul. "That's supposed to make me feel better?"

He shook his head. "I made a choice, and that hasn't changed. Janelle, I chose you. I chose us! And I chose Jaydin. What more can I do? What are you asking? For a pound of my flesh? Dammit! Lord knows I'd give it to you. I'd give you anything. I'd do anything to just make this all go away."

The way she held her cigarette up, standing tall and defiant with her lips pursed, was strangely sexy. Tucker had always been struck by her beauty, her confidence. It didn't quite make sense to him that he could be so aware of her attractiveness without feeling attracted to her. He had certainly wanted to feel the attraction. He wanted to be a normal husband and a strong, masculine role model for his son. He wanted to make his parents proud, fit in with the guys at work, all the typical things every man wanted for his life.

"I know you love me," she said. "I even think you're in love with me, at least as much as that's possible."

"I am — "

She held up her hand to silence him. "Have you slept with another man?"

His eyes locked upon hers, and though he wanted more than anything to just look away, he couldn't pull free from her gaze. He owed this to her. He had to be honest. He slowly nodded. "Yes, before we were married."

"Before we were married? And you didn't think it was worth mentioning to me?"

"I should — "

"Damn right, you should have! Jesus, Tucker!" She took another drag off her cigarette.

"I thought it was a stage. I thought...I thought I was just confused, just experimenting." He sighed, defeated. "I thought it would all just go away once we were happily married. And you know what? It did. It did go away, at least for the most part. I thought at one point I'd finally shaken the monkey from my back. I thought I'd become normal."

When the tears did begin to trickle down her cheeks, Tucker fought the urge to pull her into himself. He'd caused her all this pain, and now he just wanted to comfort her. But he couldn't. What a fucking hypocrite he'd been. What a liar.

She crushed out her cigarette and stepped toward him. "I can't imagine what you've gone through," she said, not so much as a sliver of bitterness or sarcasm in her voice. "I can't imagine your pain."

He felt his mouth drop open, then gulped and clenched his teeth together. Blinking, he fought the sting of tears behind his eyes. "No, I don't deserve compassion."

She placed her hand against his arm, ever so softly, and continued to stare into his eyes. "There's a part of me, Tucker Brown, that hates you for lying to me. But the better me knows what a wonderful man you are." She took a deep breath. "I've got to process all this. I've got to sort it out in my head and my heart, but we'll work it out. We'll work it out." She leaned in and kissed him softly on the cheek.

"Tucker, the doctor!" Janelle quickly rose to her feet.

Tucker stood to greet the doctor who quickly smiled, and before either parent could utter a word, answered the burning question. "Jaydin's doing fine. The surgery went well, and you'll be able to see him in a few minutes in the recovery room."

Chapter Two

Leaving work had never felt as wonderful as it did that morning. Ivan's twelve hour shift, which usually flew by in the blink of an eye, had dragged. It had been a long night in which the events of the previous day played out like a video in his memory. Thankfully, it had been the last of his overnights. It would be another four weeks before he had to work the graveyard duty again.

Normally, he didn't mind. The pediatric ward, generally speaking, remained peaceful. He certainly experienced less chaos when the majority of his little patients were sleeping. On the other hand, he loved his patients. He loved interacting with children, the reason he'd chosen his career in the first place.

Which, of course, was one of the things his mother had reminded him of the day prior over lunch. He'd asked her out after very careful deliberation. Ivan had already told his brother he was gay, and it had come as no surprise. As Ivan had expected, Brandon supported him a hundred percent, and he encouraged his baby bro to bite the bullet and tell their folks.

"Mom's mom," he'd said. "Of course she's gonna overreact. She's so damned dramatic, but in the end, she'll always love and accept you."

But his mother's unconditional love had never been the issue for Ivan. He knew both his parents would love and accept him no matter what, but he didn't want to hurt or disappoint either of them. Although he'd never shared their faith, he respected it. He understood they held dearly to their beliefs, and both his mom and dad were very active in their church. Sadly, it happened to be a denomination that condemned homosexuality, labeled it as an "abomination."

Appearances meant everything to Judy Ramsey. She often quoted a verse from the New Testament about abstaining from all appearance of evil. Not only was it important to her that her two boys always do the right thing, they should also constantly be aware of how their actions appeared to others.

This viewpoint, of course, sharply contrasted that of his brother Brandon, who had the attitude that people should mind their own business. Who gives a fuck what other people think? Ivan wanted to be more like his brother in this regard, but was challenged by the reality that he was a product of his mother's environment. Ivan *did* worry about what others thought. He did want people to see him as a good person, not an abomination.

Though he had never bought the religious stuff hook, line, and sinker like his parents, their conservative viewpoints on social issues had influenced him. At a time when society at large had grown more tolerant and inclusive, when gay people could now legally marry, and hundreds of celebrities lived openly, fully out of the closet, Ivan felt smothered by the bubble of his parents' outdated world view. He'd gotten beyond feeling guilty for his attractions, his masturbatory fantasies, and even his occasional thrilling yet safe hook-ups. It wasn't a guilty conscience, a presumption that he was doing something evil or immoral, but rather a knot of anxiety and sadness that rested just beneath his sternum. No, his parents wouldn't hate or disown him for being gay, but they'd certainly think less of him. They'd definitely pray for him and hope with all their hearts that he'd one day see the light and choose a normal, heterosexual lifestyle.

And, of course, this was the precise reaction Ivan's coming out had evoked from his mother. In hushed tones, leaning over her salad, she pleaded with him to think hard about how much he loved children. "Ivan, I always expected you'd be the one to give me grandchildren. You love kids so much. How are you...?" She sighed and set down her fork. "Honey, you've never even seriously dated a woman."

"Exactly." He smiled sheepishly.

"Well, how do you know if you like something if you've never even tried it?"

"Mother…" He took a sip from his water glass and placed it back on the table. "We're not talking about hummus. This isn't a 'try it, you might like it' kind of thing. And weren't you the one who always told me *not* to try sex before marriage?"

"I'm not even referring to…" She cleared her throat. "To making love. I mean you just haven't met the right girl yet."

He resisted the urge to sigh again and roll his eyes dramatically. "No, I haven't met the right girl, and that's because there is no right girl. Mother, I'm not attracted to women. I'm gay, and if there is one thing I can't stand it's when a gay guy who knows he's gay marries a woman in order to try becoming straight. I think it's about the lowest and most selfish thing a person can do. All he does is hurt other people, including the woman, the children if there are any, and all their family and friends. Eventually, it all comes out. Eventually, he has to face the reality of his own identity, who he is."

Judy glanced from left to right, obviously uncomfortable with the conversation in a public setting. "You speak of this as a matter of identity, but baby, this is not about *who* you are. It's about what you choose to do with your life. You don't *have* to be homosexual."

And you don't have to be a homophobic bitch. Rather than reply, he dabbed his mouth with his napkin. He should have anticipated this reaction. He should have known better than to take advice from his fly-by-the-seat-of-his-pants brother. Mother wasn't a "live and let live" sort of person like Brandon. Christ, Ivan wasn't either. And when his mother's eyes grew moist to the point they began to brim with tears, a sharp blade pierced Ivan's heart. This was what he hadn't wanted. This had been his greatest fear.

"Mom, I'm sorry." He reached across the table to take her hand, but she pulled away.

"Are you?" She looked him in the eyes, her own now glistening with tears.

"I waited to tell you because I didn't want this. The last thing I ever wanted to do was hurt you or Dad."

"Oh, you can't tell your father. You can *never* tell your father. It will kill him." Her voice crackled with emotion.

Ivan didn't buy it, though. He didn't look forward to coming out to his father, but he also didn't see the revelation as being too much of a shock to dear ol' Dad. Yes, he too was religious, just like Mom.   But he was so much more reserved, a very private man. He wouldn't pressure Ivan to keep looking for the right girl. He wouldn't try to guilt Ivan into complying with his desires for Ivan's life. But sadly, he too would likely feel sadness and disappointment. That was the hardest aspect of all. Ivan didn't want to hurt either of them.

"I don't know when or if I'll come out to him, but Mom, I'm not asking you to keep this a secret from him. He's your husband…"

"I'm asking *you*! Ivan, please, I beg you not to tell him. And please stop saying it like that. Coming out? What does that even mean? Coming out of the loving, protective arms of our Savior to embrace a sinful lifestyle?"

And that was pretty much the last straw. Ivan tossed his napkin onto his plate and shook his head. "I hope, Mother, that's not what you really believe. I hope you don't think that God is going to abandon me because of who I am. I hope you don't truly think that because I'm gay, I no longer am loved and protected by God." His voice had risen as had her level of discomfort. She squirmed in her chair.

"We don't have to talk about this here," she whispered.

"No, we don't. You're right." He motioned for the
waiter to bring their check. "I need to go anyway. I should try to
get a few hours sleep before my shift tonight."

After clocking out, Ivan headed to his locker. He
couldn't get the conversation with his mother out of his head. As
infuriating as she at times was, he hated leaving things unsettled
between them. Though he knew he needed to give her some
time, doing so was hard. Accepting his own identity had taken
time, and the least he owed her was the deference to process this
new reality about her son. He could logically point out that he
was the same son she'd always loved, that now she knew a little
more about him. In truth, though, his revelation had destroyed
the dream she'd had of who he was—the person she thought he
was all along. She was going to need some time to grieve the loss
of fantasy, the son she thought she had, the dream she had for
that son's life.

As he slipped his spring jacket over his scrubs, he felt
the buzz of his cell phone from his pocket. He retrieved it,
fearing for an instant it might be his mother calling. He wasn't
sure what he'd even say to her at this point. But when he looked
down at his screen, he realized he was being dialed by the
nurses' station he'd just left. Had he fucked up, forgotten
something important?

"Hello?"

"Ivan, have you left the hospital yet?" It was Carrie, his
coworker.

"No, I just punched out, and I'm at my locker. What's
up?"

"Your brother's here."

"Brandon? Oh…okay. Why?"

"He needs to talk to you. In person. Can you come back
up here right away?"

"Sure. Be right there." He ended the call, puzzled, and continued to stare at the screen a moment. Why hadn't Brandon just called him? Was there something wrong?

~ ~ ~ ~ ~

Concern and relief battled each other for control of Tucker's psyche. He'd always thought tonsillectomies were routine outpatient procedures, but Jaydin's doctor recommended they keep him overnight in the hospital due to his age and history of complications. The decision, she stressed, was merely precautionary. Having his son in the hospital worried Tucker, but on the other hand, he felt relief that the surgery had gone well and that so far he was recovering as expected.

Jaydin woke up thirsty but then complained it hurt to swallow. Annoyed, Tucker immediately asked the nurse about pain medicine. She assured him they would keep him medicated and as pain-free as possible, but that there was almost always some pain after this kind of operation. He had to drink a lot of fluids, and they'd begin giving him soft foods like ice cream and pudding as soon as he was able to tolerate them.

Tucker remained by his boy's bedside throughout the day, insisting Janelle go get a bite to eat. She brought him back a sandwich mid-afternoon, at which time Tucker finally stepped out and called Viviano.

"We're waiting on the autopsy, but everything points to homicide. Don't look like the victim died in the fire. She was already...well, looks like she took a bullet through the skull."

"Jesus." Tucker raked his fingers through his hair as he frequently did, and looked down at the sandwich on the picnic table. Pastrami, his favorite. Of course, Janelle knew exactly what he liked. "Any family?"

"Her husband, David, was away on business, and they have two adult sons, Brandon and Ivan. They all have pretty solid alibis."

"Yeah. We'll see…" Nine times out of ten these sorts of crimes were committed by immediate family, and usually the motive was money. Tucker would have to delve into every aspect of this woman's life, including her relationships with every friend or relative, before he could completely eliminate anyone as a suspect. At this point, they all were potential murderers.

"Fire stated in the bedroom. We don't have a report yet, but I talked to the fire chief. Thinks it was accelerated by gasoline. Christ, you'd think they'd try to be a little more original. Crazy. Like they're asking to get caught."

"Or stupid. Any evidence of forced entry?"

"Boss, I gotta wait on the report for that. The fire did so much damage, it's hard to tell, least by just eyeballing it."

"I'm gonna check out the scene as soon as I can, probably tomorrow morning. You got everything sealed?"

"Yeah. Tight as a drum. Take care of your kid, all right? How's the little guy doin?"

Tucker couldn't help smiling, though he was only on the phone. "He's a trooper. Keeps waking up to remind me I promised him ice cream."

"That's one sweet kid ya got there. Cute, too. Takes after his ma."

"That he does."

"Boss, don't worry. I got this. Take however much time you need for your boy, all right?"

"I'll be back tomorrow. Call and try to put a rush on that autopsy."

Viviano sighed into the phone. "I'm on it, boss. Relax."

"'kay. Call or text if you find anything out…or if you need anything."

"Good bye, boss."

"Later."

Tucker raised one leg over the picnic table bench and slid to his seat. He picked up the sandwich and sank his teeth into the soft bun. *Brandon and Ivan.* Ivan? Why'd that sound familiar? Oh, that's right. That was the name of Jaydin's nurse from this morning. Not a very common name. What were the odds of two Ivans living in Ironton? Well, if it did happen to be the same person, at least that solidified his alibi.

Of course, even when family was involved, they often didn't do the dirty work themselves. He'd do some asking around at the hospital to see if this particular Ivan was the same one in question concerning the fire. Certainly the staff would know if their coworker's mother had died in a fire, especially in a community this size.

It didn't take long to get his answer. He'd taken only his second bite of his sandwich when a couple of hospital employees emerged from the building and headed toward the outdoor furniture. "Mind if we join you?" The two young women appeared to be orderlies or nurses' aides perhaps. He smiled and nodded, inviting them to take a seat.

The one who spoke, a redhead, wore her hair pulled back away from her face. She sat next to Tucker and placed her zip-up insulated lunch cooler on the table in front of her. "Did you hear about the fire?" She directed her question to her brunette coworker who'd seated herself across from them. She then turned to Tucker. "One of the nurses here, his mother was killed in the fire."

"Really? That's horrible."

"Yeah, I was just coming in this morning when he got the news," the brunette said. "Ivan Ramsey. He usually works in pediatrics. His brother had to come here to deliver the news, and Ivan didn't take it well."

"I can only imagine." Tucker looked from one woman to the other. "Do you both know him?"

"Everyone knows Ivan." The redhead removed a bottle of water from her bag. "He's the sweetest guy here, but from what I hear, he bats for the other team."

"Sucks, don't it?" The brunette said, rolling her eyes. "It's true what they say. All the good ones are either already married or gay."

"So Ivan's gay?" As Tucker spoke, he watched the expressions on their faces. Perhaps they suddenly realized they were revealing very personal information to a complete stranger.

"Well, we don't know anything," the redhead said. "Just rumors are all they are. I'm sorry, I didn't get your name." She looked directly at Tucker, smiling.

"Tucker Brown. My son's actually a patient of that nurse. He just had a tonsillectomy."

"Oh." The brunette grew very serious. "You're not...?"

"A bigot?" He raised his eyebrows. "Not in the least. Someone very close to me happens to be gay. What were your names again?"

"I'm Cheryl," said the brunette. "And this is Brenda. We work in housekeeping, so we're in and out of almost every department. We hear all the gossip."

"You don't seem the type to gossip." He smiled.

Brenda shook her head. "I'd already heard he took it bad. My cousin works on that floor, and she's friends with Ivan. She said he had just finally come out to his mother yesterday, and she hadn't taken it well."

"Really?" Tucker leaned in.

"His parents were quite religious," Brenda continued. "Carrie, my cousin, said he had a hard time even making it through his twelve-hour shift. I guess he was really close to his mom, and he was very upset by her reaction."

"To his coming out?"

"Yeah. Like I said, she was devoutly religious. I don't think Catholic, but some fundamentalist Protestant church, I think. They don't like gays too much."

"Doesn't that family have money?" Cheryl had unwrapped a sandwich in front of her. "They lived in one of those fancy houses over in the ritzy part of town."

"His dad owned a hardware chain. Several stores. Sold it a few years back but continued to work. I guess he has a business selling lawn mowers and stuff to other hardware outlets." Brenda hadn't been exaggerating when she'd declared herself the queen of gossip. She seemed all-knowing.

"You look so familiar," she said, leaning back a bit as she examined Tucker. "You work for the police department, don't you?"

"Yes, actually." He reached into his back pocket and removed his wallet. He took out two business cards and handed one to each of the women. "I'm Detective Brown, and I'm actually going to be investigating this case. Can you do me a favor? If you hear of anything that you think might be important, can you call me?"

"Investigating? You mean, like a murder or something?" Cheryl stared at him, wide-eyed.

"Well, it's far too early to say, but every time a person dies or is killed unexpectedly, we have to look at that possibility. All I know right now was that there was a fire."

Brenda's cheeks had flushed almost to the color of her hair. "I hope…oh God, I hope I haven't said anything I shouldn't. You don't think it means anything that Ivan and his mother had that fight yesterday, do you?"

Tucker bit his bottom lip as he shrugged. "I couldn't imagine it would. You don't think so, do you?"

"No! No, of course not."

Chapter Three

The devastating tragedy hit Ivan like a high-speed locomotive. Upon receiving the news at the hospital from his brother, Ivan felt numb. It was too surreal to even process, and it didn't seem possible. But later, seeing his father face-to-face, Ivan completely lost it.

Like a rag doll, his body went limp, and he collapsed into his dad's arms, sobbing. Brandon couldn't take it. He stepped out, but Ivan's father held him tight, rocking back and forth until at last Ivan stopped trembling.

"We just had lunch together yesterday." If only he could take back the words he'd spoken. He hated knowing that she died angry and disappointed with him. "And…and…we had an argument."

"Hey." His dad pulled back, cupping Ivan's face with both hands. "Your mother loved you with all her heart, and she knew you loved her. Nothing you said could have changed that."

"I wish I'd have called her last night before work. If only…"

They were at Brandon's house, and when Ivan pulled away from his father, he turned to see who had entered behind them. It was Brandon, returning from outside, and his girlfriend Jessica was with him. She immediately embraced Ivan's father, then turned to Ivan and hugged him as well.

Had the world suddenly stopped turning? That's what it felt like to Ivan. Family members began showing up, phones were ringing, people were hugging and crying. But to Ivan it felt as if a nebulous haze surrounded him. The apocalypse had begun, and he couldn't think of a single reason to go on. Nobody had any answers. How had such a horrible thing happened? How could his mother be gone? He'd just spoken to her the day before…mere hours before her death. And now…now she was no more.

Ivan's grandparents, aunts, uncles, cousins—they all came. And every single one of them echoed the same sentiment. She was in a better place. She had gone to the arms of Jesus. The Lord had called her home, and He worked in mysterious ways. *Blah, blah, fucking blah.* By midafternoon, racked with overwhelming sadness and inexplicable grief, Ivan's sleep-deprived body collapsed onto the sofa where he dozed off, still sitting upright.

Vivid dreams of his mother swirled in his head, none of them making much sense. The gentle grasp of a hand on his shoulder and the soothing voice of his brother awakened him. Confused, he opened his eyes and looked around, then stared up into Brandon's face. "The reverend is here," he whispered.

"Oh my God, why'd you let me fall asleep?"

"You were only out about an hour, and you needed it."

The painful knot in his chest returned, accompanied by a horrific hollowness unlike anything he'd ever felt. Was this what it was like to mourn? He'd never have suspected the pain would manifest in such a physical way. All of his insides ached. He couldn't imagine consuming even a bite of food. Ever again. What was the point? Why did anything at all matter when people just died anyway?

He pushed himself up from the sofa and spun around to face Pastor Emory. Ivan had known the man most of his life, since Ivan started attending Sunday School as a preschooler. He'd always worn the same cologne, a cloying, Avon fragrance, probably sold in one of those decorative, collectible decanters. When Ivan was a child, it had reminded him of cookies, but later Ivan grew to associate it with hate.

He lost all respect for his pastor the day he delivered a fire and brimstone sermon, railing against the evils of homosexuality. The preacher had even found a translation of the New Testament somewhere that listed homosexuality as a sin so evil it warranted being cast into the Lake of Fire, the Second Death. Doctrines such as these had burdened and confused Ivan's mother. It was because of these teachings she struggled with accepting Ivan for who he was. And as Ivan approached the pastor, a wave of nausea swept over him. He had to be cordial to the man for the sake of his father, and he knew his mother would have insisted he show respect, but he didn't have to like it.

"Pastor Emory." Ivan extended his hand, but the older man moved closer, immediately pulling Ivan into his embrace. "I'm so sorry for your loss."

"Thank you." What else was there to say? How did one respond to these expressions of condolence? Nothing came to mind that sounded sincere in Ivan's head. He certainly wasn't thankful that people were sorry, and why were they sorry in the first place? They had nothing to apologize for. *Strange, our choice of words at such poignant times in our existence.*

"But she is now in the hands of our loving Savior. Ivan, your mother is this day in Paradise."

Oh Christ, must he quote from the Crucifixion story? These were the words Jesus spoke to the dying thief who hung on the cross alongside him. Did this so-called man of God truly believe his cliché expressions offered any comfort?

Ivan stepped back, shocked by his own cynicism. It wasn't like him to feel such anger and bitterness. Yet in the moment, fury roiled within him. He wanted to ask the pastor why. He wanted to demand an explanation of God. How could he have allowed such a horrendous thing to happen? And he wanted to reach out and smack the man for spouting platitudes and meaningless, trite sayings at a time like this, a time of horrific sadness.

Instead, Ivan smiled and nodded. "Yes, she had tremendous faith."

"I understand there is so much to process right now, and you all must allow yourselves time to mourn." The reverend looked into the face of Ivan's father, then back to Ivan and Brandon. "But sometime within the next twenty-four to thirty-six hours, we need to discuss the memorial."

"Can we come to the church tomorrow morning?" Ivan's father bore a stern, sober expression.

"Of course, or I can come here. Whatever you prefer."

"I have to meet with the funeral director in the morning around nine. We will come to the church afterward."

"If possible, bring any photos you'd like us to use. Or if you have a special poem or song, anything you want included in the service."

How could they be thinking of these things so soon? Ivan wrapped his arms around his abdomen. "If you'll excuse me." He turned and headed down the hall to the bathroom. He was going to be sick.

Once inside, he slammed the door and slid to his knees in front of the toilet. Doubling over, he lowered his head and wretched. It had been hours since he'd eaten, but his abdominal muscles convulsed, forcing acrid bile from his gut into his throat. He heaved into the toilet, no more than a couple tablespoons of putrid liquid. Then the dry heaves commenced. Over and over, he gagged, but he had nothing left within him to expel. Weak and exhausted, he slumped over, curling onto the floor in a fetal position.

"Ivan, are you all right?" Brandon stood on the other side of the door, trying vainly to gain entry. Ivan was blocking the door. "Please let me in, man."

Ivan's cheeks were now streaked with tears. Had he been crying from grief, or were his eyes merely watering from the violent spasms his body had just experienced? It didn't matter. It all hurt the same. The hollowness within him expanded, consuming him, and a fierce onslaught of emotion swept over him. He couldn't have stopped himself from sobbing even if he'd tried. The deafening cry that erupted from his vocal chords was primal and shrill. His soul had been rendered, and this was its shriek of protest.

Pulling his knees toward his chest, his legs moved away from the door just enough for Brandon to push it open. Forcing his way in, he slid onto his knees beside his baby brother, pulling Ivan into his protective embrace. "It's okay." Brandon's voice broke with emotion. "It's okay, man. Let it out. Let it out." He rocked his brother in his arms, and Ivan clung to him, pressing his face against Brandon's chest. He had to feel his warmth, hear his heartbeat. He had to gain assurance that his brother was still with him. Still alive.

~ ~ ~ ~ ~

Tucker had sacrificed his three days of custody to Janelle that week. They'd agreed it would be in Jaydin's best interest to have a full week of recovery with his mother. Tucker would make up the time soon, after his son was feeling better, and would take him an entire week. Jaydin's first night home from the hospital, Tucker slept over, using Janelle's sofa as a bed.

"Did you find anything out about the fire?" They'd just tucked Jaydin in for the night, and he was sleeping peacefully. Janelle handed her ex-husband a beer across the bar that separated the kitchen and dining room area.

"Thanks." He took a swig and leaned against the wall behind him. "I visited the crime site today. There's not much left, the house a total loss. It's going to be difficult, if not impossible, to get much physical evidence."

"How do you know it wasn't an accidental fire?" She stepped around the bar and headed toward the archway leading into the living room. Tucker followed her.

"Oh, the fire department is able to tell almost immediately if a fire has been set. Not to mention, the victim was likely already dead when the fire started. She'd been shot."

Janelle stopped in her tracks and turned around. "No shit?" She retrieved her cigarette pack from its hiding place.

"I hope you're not gonna start smoking again."

She flashed him a dirty look and placed a hand on her hip. "Our son has asthma. Of course, I'm not going to start again."

He stared at the Newports in her hand.

"Just cut me some slack. One cigarette every day or two is my only vice."

"You know that nurse who was with Jay Jay till he went in for surgery? Ivan, I think. It was his mother who died in that fire."

"Oh my God." Her mouth dropped open in astonishment. "So yesterday when he was with us, prepping Jay for surgery, his mom was already dead and he didn't even know it?"

Tucker nodded. "And he's gay, ya know."

Her expression morphed to one of puzzlement. "And what's that have to do with anything?"

Tucker shrugged. "Just sayin."

She walked across the living room to the sliding glass door and slid it open, then stepped onto the patio. "You think he's cute, don't you?"

He moved closer to her, crossing the threshold onto the cement patio. "Don't be ridiculous. Of course not. He's a suspect."

"Maybe." She smiled. "And maybe a cute suspect at that."

Tucker tried to appear incredulous, but he felt a tad annoyed she'd so easily seen through him. Of course, he'd noticed how attractive Ivan was. Jesus Christ, the guy was like sex on legs. He'd have had to be blind not to notice someone like that.

"And how can he even be a suspect?" She took a drag from her cigarette, exhaling slowly. "You already know he was working all night."

"The entire immediate family are all suspects until eliminated. He just happens to be a suspect with a pretty solid alibi. Doesn't mean anything, though. You don't have to be present at the time a crime is committed to be responsible for it."

"You're not fooling me, Tuck." She laughed, waving one hand dismissively. "You know that nurse didn't kill anyone. And you might as well admit he's a hottie. I saw the way you were checking him out."

He took another swig of beer. "Even if there was no conflict of interest, he's not my type."

"He is totally your type. Tuck, Ivan is the epitome of your type."

Tucker nearly guffawed. "Whatever."

"He's smart, sexy, has a great job, and he loves children. What more is there?"

"Why're you giving me advice anyway? You should be focused on finding a man of your own.

"I already have a little man. His name's Jay Jay."

"Yeah, me too." Tucker walked to edge of the patio and stared out at the cloudless sky. The stars were out and seemed to shine brighter than normal. "At a time like this, I doubt that nurse is going to be interested in any man. He just lost his mother."

"Well, maybe this is the perfect time to forge a new friendship."

"Like I said, there's a conflict of interest." He turned to look at her. "I can't be a friend to anyone in that family right now. I have a job to do."

She slid into one of the patio chairs, crossing her legs at the knee. "When you go in for a beer, be a dear and grab my wine glass. I left it on the counter." He tilted back his head as he raised the beer bottle to his lips and drained it.

"All right. I do think you're right about one thing, though. I don't think Ivan Ramsey is a murderer."

~ ~ ~ ~ ~

For the next week, Ivan functioned on auto-pilot. There was so much to do, so many things Ivan's father needed help navigating. Although his parents had already made final arrangements, they still had to plan the funeral. Ivan had to pull himself together and be strong for his dad's sake. He'd had his moment, his complete breakdown. His mother, of all people, would want him to remain stoic going forward. She'd expect him to face tragedy with a degree of dignity. She'd always concerned herself with appearances, and the last thing she'd want would be for her son to lose it in public.

He allowed himself to go numb and suppress his intense emotions. It was the only strategy that allowed him to greet and thank so many people who'd reached out to the family with expressions of condolence.

With his parents being so active in the church, the entire congregation seemed to be involved in the memorial. For the most part, the church ladies were very sweet, and they all had very kind words for Ivan and his family. They also had no concept of moderation, at least when it came to food. They not only prepared massive quantities of casseroles, sandwiches, salads, and desserts for the memorial, but they delivered equally as much food to Brandon's house.

And after the closed-casket service and the interment, Ivan's father faced a mountain of paperwork. They had death certificates to obtain, creditors to contact, insurance companies to notify. The home owner's insurance was the worst. His father had lost everything, and they had to try to compile an inventory and determine replacement costs on every item. That process would have been painful enough in and of itself, but the death of his mother made it all the worse. Every detail — every physical item lost — was tied to a memory.

As horrific as the process was, Ivan felt a twisted sense of appreciation for all the busy work. It allowed him to remain focused upon his mom. The obvious challenges they faced during their time of transition at the very least gave Ivan pause, allowed him to think about how complex life was and how many people were touched by the life of one individual. Had she simply been buried and forgotten, had life just gone on as normal, Ivan wasn't sure he'd have been able to cope. He welcomed the turmoil and chaos and viewed them as proof that his mother's life had mattered.

But when a police detective showed up, and a member of the media cornered Ivan, Brandon, and their father one morning at a restaurant, asking questions about how Mrs. Ramsey had died, Ivan became concerned. And annoyed.

"What was she talking about?" Ivan sat across from his father at the local diner. Ivan turned to his brother. "That reporter, what did she mean? It was a fire. An accident."

"Apparently, they're not sure it was an accident." Brandon took a sip of his water.

"Of course it was an accident." Ivan stared directly at his father. "And why'd that detective contact me? He wants me to meet him for an interview."

David Ramsey leaned back, straightening his posture in the chair as he scrubbed a hand across his face. "I didn't want to tell you everything yet… I mean, until I knew for sure. But there was an autopsy conducted. Routine, really. And the fire was determined not to be the cause of death."

"What?" Ivan leaned forward, elbows on the table. "What the hell, Dad? What are you saying?"

His father looked at him sternly, perhaps in response to Ivan's language. He took a deep breath. "Sorry, I didn't tell you because…It was just too much to deal with."

"Dad, how did she die then?" Brandon's tone was more measured.

"Apparently she was shot."

"Shot!" Ivan and Brandon spoke in unison.

"The police think someone killed your mother and then set the fire to try covering it up."

"No!" Ivan shook his head. "This is crazy. Why? Why would someone do that?"

"That's why they want to talk to all of us," Brandon surmised. "They want to find out which one of us had a motive to kill our own mother."

David raised one hand. "Now just a minute. Hold on, and quit…" He took a deep breath. "Try not to get emotional about this. The police are just doing their job. They know someone killed your mother, and they have to question everyone. Of course, they're going to start with us first. Once we are eliminated as suspects — "

"Suspects?" Ivan nearly shouted. "Why would someone kill my mother? And why on earth would they ever suspect Brandon or me…or *you*." He stared at his father.

"Well, of course we didn't kill your mother. It had to have been a burglary or something. Someone broke into the house. Lord knows why. We have no idea what, if anything, they took. It's not like we can take an inventory at this point. But whoever did it probably killed your mom to keep her from identifying them."

"And to get away," Brandon added.

"Right." David looked into Ivan's eyes as he reached across the table and placed one hand on his son's wrist. "The police are just doing their job. Just cooperate with them, because we want more than anyone for this monster to be caught. The sooner they clear our family, the sooner they can find the killer."

Ivan again felt as if he'd been body-slammed. The news was unfathomable. It sounded like an episode of Forensic Files or NCIS. This shit didn't happen in real life. Not to him and his family.

After lunch, Ivan excused himself, saying he needed to head back to his apartment. When he got to his car he retrieved a business card from his pocket that Detective Viviano had left him. "This is my partner's card. He's leading the investigation. Detective Brown." Ivan stared at the card, trying to recall why the name sounded so familiar. He dialed the number.

"Detective Brown."

"Hello, this is Ivan Ramsey. Your partner left me your card and said I needed to contact you."

"Oh yes. Hello, Ivan. Thanks for returning my call. I just need to talk to you about—"

"About who killed my mother."

"Yes, I'm so sorry for your loss."

"Look, I don't appreciate your insinuations. I know you think someone in our family did it, but that's utter bullshit."

"No, I don't assume anything like that."

"And don't you think my father has enough to deal with at a time like this? Shouldn't you be out looking for the murderer instead of harassing us? We're the victims here."

"I want to catch the murderer more than anything, but in order to do that, I need your cooperation. Like I said, I'm sorry. I wish there was some other way."

"I'll come in right now for your interview."

"That would be wonderful. Or I could meet you somewhere."

"I'll come to the police station. I'll answer your questions, but then I want this to be over with. I want you to catch my mother's killer and quit wasting time."

"That's the plan."

"Good!" Ivan ended the call.

Chapter Four

Did Ivan Ramsey even know who he'd been talking to on the phone? No, of course he didn't. Why would he? Just because Tucker hadn't been able to get the young man out of his head since that day almost two weeks ago when Jaydin had his surgery, didn't mean that Ivan would give Tucker a second thought. And with all that had happened to that family in recent days, thoughts of a semi-closeted, divorced, gay cop would be the furthest thing from Ivan's mind.

If only Tucker could put Ivan out of his own mind. For whatever reason, he found himself thinking about the young man frequently. Well, to be fair, he was supposed to be thinking about him. Tucker's job was to solve the mystery of Ivan's mother's death. Tucker needed to remain focused on not only Ivan, but the entire family. He needed to find a link, if there was one, to the murderer. Either one of the family members themselves or someone they associated with was likely responsible.

Though in theory it was possible a stranger had burglarized the home, killed Mrs. Ramsey, then torched the place, it was unlikely. Most cases like this proved to be inside jobs. The key to piecing the puzzle together was to learn as much as possible from every individual associated with the victim, then follow the right leads.

Without even talking directly with Ivan, Tucker had all but eliminated him as a suspect. Everything about his demeanor, according to the accounts by family and friends of his reaction to his mother's death, told Tucker that Ivan had been floored by his mother's unexpected passing. Even his defensiveness on the phone, his natural tendency to protect and defend his family, suggested he harbored intense familial loyalty. Yes, he'd argued with his mother the day before her murder, but the very nature of that conversation indicated how close they were and that he wanted to maintain this relationship with his mom. He'd opened up to her, told her he was gay. If the conversation hadn't gone well, as apparently it hadn't, Ivan would not likely strike out with vengeance. He'd likely retreat. He'd probably pull away from her to allow her time but never completely give up on gaining her acceptance and understanding.

Was this really the case, or was Tucker projecting? He remembered how difficult it had been to come out to his own family. Fortunately, both his folks were amazingly supportive. They didn't live nearby, but they'd been thrilled when Tucker got engaged, and they'd been involved long-distance in the life of their grandchild. In spite of all she'd been through with Tucker, his mom told him that his coming out of the closet was not nearly as big a shock to her as he'd expected it to be. Frankly, she said, she'd been more surprised by his engagement to Janelle. Not because she was Black, but because she was female.

It didn't at first make a whole lot of sense to Tucker. He wasn't exactly the gay stereotype. He didn't listen to a lot of show tunes or gesture with campy hand movements and wrist flops. He'd never had any desire to dress in drag, hated shopping, and knew nothing about interior decorating. He was in every way the cliché "straight-acting" gay dude. So how had his mother known about him? She said it was an intuition, something she'd just always sensed.

Apparently all mothers did not possess this sixth sense when it came to picking up on their child's sexual orientation. Maybe it was a gift only bestowed on some mothers, or maybe it was a characteristic that many parents chose to ignore. It didn't seem as predominant among fathers as it was with mothers, but this came as no surprise. Women overall were more in touch with their emotions. They could pick up on signals unspoken that men often overlooked. Hopefully Tucker would learn to open himself up enough to tap into this sort of empathy when it came to his son. No matter what Jaydin's sexual orientation or gender identity was, he wanted to support his child a hundred percent.

When the dispatcher at the front desk dialed him at his cubicle, Tucker took a deep breath and steeled himself for the interview. He rose from his chair and made his way down the hallway to greet Ivan Ramsey. As he stepped around the partition and locked his gaze upon Ivan's face, Tucker was taken aback momentarily. The vibrant blue in Ivan's eyes seemed to penetrate Tucker's soul, and as Ivan stood there defiantly, his air of confidence ignited something within Tucker. An inexplicable thrill coursed through Tucker's frame, tingling down his limbs, and he thought for a second he was going to pop a boner judging from the tightness in his pants. But he took another deep breath and cleared his throat, ignoring the natural reactions of his body. He had a job to do, and that's all there was to it.

"Ivan, I'm Detective Brown."

Ivan's eyes opened wider and the corners of his mouth curled up just a bit into what seemed like a smirk. "You're Jaydin's dad. I remember you. You were late for your son's surgery."

"Guilty." Tucker nodded. "To be honest, I was late because I'd gotten called to the fire. I'm sorry I didn't realize at the time…"

"Yeah, me too."

"You want to come back to a conference room? We can talk about this a little more easily there…in private."

"So you can record me without me knowing? Have someone watch me through two-way glass?"

Tucker smiled. "Nothing as formal as all that. I'm just gathering information at this point. I want you to know, we're on the same team here. We want to find the responsible party, right?"

"I'm not on any team." Ivan tightened his jaw and squared his shoulders. "Well, let's go then."

Tucker led the way back down the hall to a small conference room. There were, in fact, cameras mounted in each corner of the tiny room. Tucker quickly pointed them out, explaining they were surveillance cameras. "We can go to a different location, if you're more comfortable. We can go over to the diner or outside…"

"No, this is fine." Ivan took a seat at the folding table. "I don't have anything to hide. Go on, ask your questions." He folded his arms across his chest.

"Well, apparently you're already aware that the cause of your mother's death wasn't related to the fire."

"I just found out from my dad. Moments ago."

"I'm sorry."

Ivan scowled. "Who would do something like this?"

"Do you know of anyone who was unhappy with your mother? Did she have any enemies you were aware of?"

"Enemies?" Ivan laughed sardonically. "You can't be serious. My mom's been a member of women's church guild for the past two decades. She organized the bake sales for the missionary fund, taught Sunday School, and volunteered for Vacation Bible School every summer. And it wasn't just the church she was involved in. She was a Cub Scout den mother when Brandon and I were young. She used to be on the PTA. She's sponsored every imaginable charitable event from the Alzheimer's walk to the Breast Cancer Relay for Life. No, she didn't have enemies! Everyone loved my mom. Everyone!"

"Did you ever see her become angry or get into an argument with anyone?" Tucker kept his tone even, unfazed by Ivan's emotion.

"She was a human being, ya know." The timbre in Ivan's voice rose slightly. "Of course she got angry. But no, I don't remember her arguing with anyone. She didn't even argue with my dad. That just wasn't her. She was all about..." he sighed.

"About what?"

"She was concerned a lot about appearances. She would never make a scene. Never. So no, she didn't have enemies."

"Anyone you know of who disliked her? Falsely accused her? Threatened her?"

"No! No, don't you think I'd have reported that already?"

"Ivan, do you own any handguns?"

Ivan stared at him a moment, his mouth opening slightly. His eyes grew wide with an incredulous stare. "Are you serious? You're asking me if *I* own a gun? What the hell? Do you think...?"

"I don't think anything. I'm asking because I have to ask everyone. Ivan, do you own a handgun?"

"No, I don't own a fucking handgun! I don't own any guns."

"What about your family?"

"Well, ya know, I'd think you'd already have that figured out. There was a fire and everything was burnt, the place utterly gutted. I'm sure you already know my dad had a gun cabinet with guns in it. What kind, I have no idea. I've never been into guns."

"So your father owns guns. What about your brother, Brandon?"

"Brandon didn't kill our mother, and neither did my dad!"

"Do you know if Brandon owns a handgun?"

"I don't know! Maybe…*probably*. Our whole family…we were raised to believe in the Second Amendment. It's not a crime to own a gun. That doesn't make a person a murderer."

Tucker reached down and removed his holster, placing his weapon beside him on the table. "I'm a believer in the Second Amendment myself. Ivan, please relax. This isn't an inquisition."

"You could've fooled me. It sure feels like one!" His eyes were becoming moist. Damn, Tucker hadn't wanted to reduce him to tears.

"Let's change the subject, okay? Tell me about you. I know you're a nurse at St. Joe's."

Ivan reached up to rub his eyes with each index finger, then looked at Tucker. "I guess I'm going to have to tell you something about myself, something that's none of your business, but I know you're going to find out anyway…if you haven't already."

Tucker leaned back, resting his forearms on his chair's armrests. He raised his eyebrows.

"My mom and I had words the day before she died, not exactly an argument. More of a disagreement."

"Okay."

"See…" He took a deep breath. "She was always a person of faith, deeply religious. And it concerned her when Brandon and I didn't live our lives the way she thought we should — the way she thought God would want us to."

"So she was unhappy about a lifestyle choice you've made."

If looks could kill, Tucker would've been dead. "No, it's not a choice!" The way Ivan's face scrunched all up when he scowled almost made Tucker burst out laughing. "I mean, what we talked about. It wasn't anything about my choices…well, not really."

"You don't have to tell me all this." Tucker leaned forward. "I want to find out who killed your mother, Ivan. I don't think you did it, but I think you can be a big help to us in this investigation."

"W-wait. If you don't think someone in my family is guilty, then what's the point of this questioning?"

"I haven't been able to officially rule anyone out as a suspect. I'm just being straight with you. In my professional opinion, you don't fit the profile. You have no motive. You have no weapon."

"Well, you already established there were weapons in the house. I could have used one of them."

Tucker couldn't help himself. He smiled as Ivan sat across from him glaring petulantly. "Well, I suppose…"

"Has anyone ever told you that you come across as a smug asshole?" Ivan crossed his arms over his chest again.

Tucker shrugged. "My ex-wife a few times."

"You should listen to her. She seems like a brilliant woman. Look, since I'm not a suspect, mind if I leave?"

"Ivan, I'm sorry. I didn't mean to offend you." Tucker rose from his chair as Ivan shot up and spun around to face the exit. He stepped to the door, then turned his head in Tucker's direction. "Call me when you have some actual information…or if you have a real question for me. And for God's sake, please quit wasting time harassing me and my family. There's a killer on the loose somewhere."

He didn't wait for Tucker to respond, but pulled open the door and stormed down the hall.

Tucker made no attempt to stop him.

~ ~ ~ ~ ~

43

Ivan's dad had been staying with Brandon and Jessica since the fire but had finally decided he needed to get away for a while. Ivan's parents had purchased a timeshare in Florida where they vacationed every winter for two weeks. David offered to take Ivan with him, but Ivan hadn't yet accrued enough vacation time. Plus, he needed to immerse himself in work. He loved his job, and as painful as his mother's passing had been, he had to go on with his life. She'd have wanted him to do exactly that. She'd have insisted.

Now on day shift, he'd just completed his three day stretch of twelve-hour shifts. Well, they called them twelve-hour shifts, but in reality they were usually thirteen or fourteen hours. It was now Friday evening and he had the next two days off. He'd promised himself he'd do something that wasn't depressing. He'd shed enough tears, spent hours looking through family photos on Facebook and Shutterly, remembering his mom. Although all her family pictures had been lost in the fire, she had painstakingly and fastidiously scanned and uploaded all the old print pictures, preserving them in digital format. He and Brandon had teased her at the time. *Nobody does that, Mom.* But she had.

Carrie had suggested he come over for a movie night on Saturday and he probably would. She had a little girl whom Ivan adored, and Carrie's husband was about the least homophobic straight guy Ivan had ever known. Well, other than Brandon maybe.

He'd known Carrie since college. They went through the nursing program together and had been best friends ever since. She remained the one person in whom he was comfortable enough to confide anything. She'd known he was gay before he started coming out to any of his other friends or family. And she'd been there for him when Liam had dumped him, or when he'd dumped Liam. However you chose to look at it.

God, how had he gotten involved with a guy like Liam in the first place? The two were polar opposites. Liam majored in political science and was a conservative. He viewed everything in terms of the bottom line, in black and white. Sex was sex, and it shouldn't be confused with emotion or intimacy. Liam didn't cuddle. He wasn't the type who spoke terms of endearment. And he wasn't even a baby step out of the closet.

In many ways, Liam's core values had mirrored Ivan's mother's. He too concerned himself with appearances, though if you were to point this out to him, he'd vehemently deny it. He said he didn't give a shit what other people thought of him and projected a cocky air of self-confidence, yet Ivan always suspected it to be a veneer. If anything, Liam had been terrified of other people judging him.

Their politics didn't mesh, but so what? Ivan's parents had been rock rib Republicans his entire life, and that really didn't bother him. Had Liam been one of those Log Cabin members, they might have had their disagreements, but at least Ivan would've been able to respect the principles on which Liam stood. Instead, Liam was very open about his conservative political views, but he kept his sexual orientation a deep, dark secret.

In private, Liam made the argument to Ivan that his personal life was no one else's business. He did not feel the need to flaunt being gay, to "shove it down anyone's throat." *You had no problem shoving it down mine last night.* But Ivan generally didn't waste his breath arguing. He'd hoped that in time Liam would evolve. Eventually he'd begin to come out of the closet and allow Ivan to share all of his life as his partner and not just his "roommate."

But that day never came. The spring of their senior year Liam announced he'd taken a job in D.C, an offer he couldn't refuse. But when Ivan offered to apply for some positions in Washington and Maryland, Liam brushed him off. "I don't think that's a good idea."

Ivan, standing at the bathroom sink in their dorm room, turned and stared at him, astonished. "What do you mean? How are we going to…?"

"I think we should maybe think about seeing other people." Liam sat on his bed, computer in his lap, and didn't even bother to look up at Ivan.

"What?"

"I mean, well…" He finally raised his head to glance over at Ivan. "You know I'm going to have to get married someday, right?"

"Yeah, of course. But I guess you mean to someone other than me?"

"I mean *really* married. To a woman. If for no other reason than for my career. There might be a way we can still see each other on the side, though. Maybe we could figure something out."

Ivan stood there, paralyzed, and his jaw nearly hit the floor. "Liam, hasn't the past two and a half years meant anything to you?"

Liam sighed, then looked back at his laptop monitor. "Let's not talk about it now. We'll work it out."

Ivan worked it out for them. He packed up and moved out. He moved back to his parents and commuted for his finals. He then landed the job at St. Joseph's which was where he'd been interning. He hadn't seen or heard from Liam since graduation. He worked for some high-powered Senator now.

Since then, Ivan hadn't gotten serious with any guy. He'd barely dated. His bizarre work schedule didn't help, but beside that, he wasn't ready to have his heart shattered again. The worst thing about his disastrous relationship with Liam was that he hadn't really even been able to talk to anyone about it. Only a handful of friends from school knew about them. But he wasn't in school anymore, and he hadn't come out to his family yet. Thankfully, he'd had Carrie.

As he pulled his vehicle into his carport, Ivan cursed himself for not stopping somewhere for takeout. He had nothing in the fridge. Maybe he'd order delivery. Or maybe he could call Dustin, his one gay friend. If Dustin didn't have a show tonight, he might want to catch a bite with Ivan and head over to Extasy afterward for a couple drinks.

Dustin, aka Miss Dusty, lived in Ivan's apartment building. He...or *she*...did drag and was the most glamorous and hilarious drag queen Ivan had ever known. Well, to be honest, she was the *only* drag queen he knew personally. They had no romantic connection but had become close over the previous two years since Dustin moved in.

As Ivan stepped out of his car and closed the door behind him, he fished his cell phone from his scrub pocket. But before he could ring Dustin, he heard his name. He spun around to face the very friend he was about to dial.

"Hey, man, I was just about to call you."

"Doll, you have a long day?" Dustin walked briskly across the concrete, sashaying with heels clicking all the way, and placed his hand on Ivan's shoulder.

"All my days are long." Ivan smiled and sighed. "And I'm starving. Want to go grab dinner? My treat."

Dustin raised his hand to his chest, barely touching the cleft of his pectorals with his fingertips. "It must be fate. The gods have destined us to dine together because I was just on my way to get Chinese takeout."

"Have you ordered already?"

He shook his head. "Oh no, I never call ahead. I like to wait there and flirt with the cute Asian guy at the counter. Sum yung hung guy."

"Figures." Ivan smiled. "Let me get changed real quick. Come on, you can have a drink while you wait."

"Sugar, I can help you change. Won't take me but a second to get you out of those scrubs. Unless," he raised a finger to his chin as if thinking. "Unless you want to just keep them on and give me an examination." He winked.

"I'm too hungry to think about cock right now. Come on." He took a step down the sidewalk and motioned for Dustin to follow.

Dustin's bottom lip protruded slightly. "All I get from you is rejection."

"And free food."

"That too." He smiled and skipped to catch up. "You must *really* be hungry!"

Chapter Five

Before Tucker could even walk around the car and get the backseat door open, Jaydin had his seat belt unfastened. Damn, he was growing up so fast. Though fiercely independent and usually insistent upon walking, he allowed his daddy to pick him up and carry him into the house. Tucker scooped up his son's backpack and slung it over his other shoulder.

The front door opened, and Jaydin began blabbering to his mommy about all that he and Daddy had done the previous three days. She leaned in and kissed him on the forehead, then smiled at her ex-husband. "Have you eaten? You're welcome to join us. I'm grilling burgers on the patio."

"Mommy, I want nuggets!"

"You just had nuggets for lunch," Tucker reminded him.

"I want 'em again. I don't like ham boogers."

"You can have a hot dog," Janelle suggested. "And watermelon."

"Watermelon? Yay!"

Tucker set Jaydin down and looked at his ex-wife. "I'd better not. I have a ton of work." He handed her Jaydin's backpack. "He needs a refill on his inhaler. I called it in to the doctor. Just needs to be picked up at the pharmacy. If you don't have time—"

"I'll get it in the morning. Did he need his inhaler? Why didn't you call me?" Her face crinkled with concern.

"Just once. No big deal."

"Tucker, damn it." She stared at him, obviously frustrated.

"Mommy, don't be mad." Jaydin wrapped his arm around his mother's leg. "Daddy helped me. He knows how to do the haler."

"I thought we'd agreed you'd let me know if he had an attack."

Tucker took a deep breath. "It was very minor. I'm sorry I didn't call you."

"I'm big now!" Jaydin looked up at his mother. "I can do it all by myself. Sort of."

"I know honey." She squatted down, lowering herself to his eye-level. "Mommy's just being silly, a worrywart as usual."

Tucker actually *had* almost called her. He'd held the phone in his hand ready to press his thumb on the call button, but had changed his mind. They shared joint custody, and he was equally responsible for his son's health and safety. She didn't call Tucker every single time Jaydin had a breathing problem. And what good would it do to call her? She'd just worry unnecessarily.

Sometimes he wondered if he'd made the right decision. Maybe it would have been best for everyone if he'd never come out to Janelle. Or maybe they should have just agreed to continue living in the same house for Jaydin's sake. But at the time, it felt like the right thing to do. He wanted his ex-wife to get on with her life, meet someone and find happiness. That would never happen with the two of them living under the same roof.

And he thought maybe—just *maybe*—he'd meet someone, too. Over the previous twelve months, since he'd gotten his own place, Tucker had gone on a couple dates, but they didn't turn into anything. He might never find another gay guy who'd be interested in a relationship with a man like him, a cop and a father. Jaydin would always be his priority. He'd always have to come first, no matter what. Not many people—male or female—could accept that.

"You're going to work all weekend, aren't you?" Janelle knew him like the back of her hand. Of course, he'd be focused on work all weekend. What else was there for him to do? Plus, he had a full boat when it came to caseload, the Ramsey file first and foremost in his mind. Some of the pieces were beginning to come together, but he didn't yet have enough evidence to proceed.

"You should take the night off, go out with some friends or something. Go have a drink." She stood with one hand on her hip and looked at him as if she were reading a billboard. How did she do that? How was she able to read his mind…and emotions…so well?

He laughed sarcastically. "Yeah, right. I have so many friends calling I can't fit them all into my busy social calendar."

"Well, you big dummy. There's a reason why you don't have friends. You have to go out and meet people. You know — show yourself friendly." Was that a Bible verse she just quoted?

"Mommy! Daddy's not a dummy."

"Mommy's only teasing." She reached down to ruffle the little boy's hair.

"No, your mommy's right. Daddy can be a dummy sometimes. But she should also take her own advice." He raised his eyebrows as he glanced at Janelle. She was no better than him in this regard. She worked full time, focused all her attention on Jaydin. He didn't think she had any more of an overbooked social calendar than he had.

"Touché."

He took a deep breath, then lowered himself to kiss and hug his son goodbye. "You be good for Mommy. I'll be here Monday night to pick you up."

"Okay, Daddy. Can we get ice cream?"

He smiled in spite of a futile attempt to remain serious. "I'll think about it. But we just got ice cream last night."

"I know! A long time ago."

As he slipped behind the wheel of his all-too-practical four-door sedan, Tucker looked back to the house before backing out of the driveway. He'd made a choice to give up this life in order to be true to himself and to be honest with his ex-wife and son. He'd thought they'd all be happier once he laid everything out in the open and pursued a life in which he'd felt complete. But *this* was also part of who he was. Yeah, he was a gay man. He emotionally, socially, and sure-as-fuck physically connected with other men, but he also liked being a dad. He also liked having a family life.

He pulled away and thought about the case he was working on. *Ivan Ramsey*. Tucker really shouldn't be thinking about him as much as he was. Though the young man's attractiveness couldn't be denied, Tucker wasn't even in the guy's league. He was obviously educated. He had a nursing degree and seemed very smart. And he clearly knew about fashion and always looked stunning. Quick-witted, very confident in who he was, and probably most appealing of all — he had a streak of cockiness. He didn't seem a bit intimidated by Tucker's position of authority.

Ivan also cared about family — at least he seemed to. He defended his father and brother, and spoke very highly of his mother even after she'd rejected him when he came out to her. Tucker didn't know how he'd have handled it had his own parents reacted this way to his orientation. And Ivan also possessed an amazing talent when it came to relating to children. Tucker had seen him in action, seen him with Jaydin.

He shook his head. How stupid of him to allow his thoughts to constantly drift back to this topic. *This person*. It was probably just a case of gay cabin fever. He lived in a small community where there weren't a whole lot of gay people, certainly not single, twentysomething *male* gay people. It stood to reason Tucker would notice how attractive the guy was. Who wouldn't? Maybe Janelle was right. Maybe he needed to go out and relax a bit, make some new friends.

He hadn't been back to the only gay bar in the county since the one time two years ago when Janelle had found out about him. What would it hurt for him to go and hang out a bit, check things out? Maybe he'd meet someone...maybe just for conversation. Or more. Maybe then he'd get his mind off the one person who was practically driving him crazy.

He nodded resolutely. That's what he'd do. He'd go to Extasy and forget all about Ivan Ramsey.

~ ~ ~ ~ ~

"Why'd I bother having them box this up?" Ivan laughed as he placed the takeout containers on the floor of the back seat. "Now I have to carry this shit around in my car."

"Trust me, you'll thank yourself later. Leftover Chinese is the best after-sex binge food."

"As if." He closed the door and opened the front driver's side, then slid behind the wheel. Dustin had already seated himself shotgun.

"See, right there's your problem."

"What?" Ivan stared at him, feigning ignorance.

"Your fucking attitude. My dear, you've become so cynical." He held out his hand, examining his nails. "Fuck, I need a mani...*bad*."

"Well, I *don't* need a manny. I have way too much emotional bullshit going on right now. Too much to deal with." He slid the key into the ignition and started the car.

"A *manicure*, bonehead. And you *do* need a manny, actually. With a big cocky to fuck your booty. That's what you *need*. A good, hard fuck. Trust me, there ain't a problem in the world a nice stiff cock can't solve."

Ivan sighed. "I'd settle for a few stiff drinks right now." He grew serious as he pulled out of the parking lot. "This is the first time I've been out since..."

"I know, sweetie, which is why you're going to have a good time tonight, get your ass wasted, and then get yourself laid. You need to let go of all this sadness and enjoy yourself. You know she wouldn't want you wallowing around, all sad and mopey all the time."

"True." He glanced over to his friend, offering a sincere yet meek smile. "But on the other hand, my mother wasn't overjoyed to find out I was gay."

Dustin's head twitched just a bit. He reached up to brush hair away from his face, and then he too grew serious. "I'm sorry, Ivan. You know, the timing of that whole thing really sucks. You coming out, I mean, right before the…um, accident. But can I ask you something?"

"Sure."

"I didn't know your mother, never met her, so I can't say everything would have eventually been just fine between you too. I mean, look at me. I haven't spoken to my folks in the last six years. They've disowned me. But because you were so close to your mom, what do you think? Do you think she would have come around and finally accepted you, supported you for who you really are…given more time?"

Ivan stared straight ahead at the lines on the road. After thinking for a moment, he nodded. "I really do." His voice was barely a whisper. "I think she'd have gone on to become my biggest ally. I think, even though it would've been hard at first, she'd have decided that God made me who I am."

Dustin smiled, then reached over to place his hand on Ivan's thigh. "There you go, then. That's what you need to think about. Stop clinging to the painful memory. You've let yourself obsess on a single conversation you had with your mom, but in reality, it would have been only the first of many talks you'd have with each other. You knew and loved her with your whole heart. You know she would never abandon or condemn you. She loved you too much."

The emotion returned, and Ivan had to blink away tears. He didn't want his grief to ruin the first night he'd had out with a friend in months, but he couldn't quite conquer the guilt that kept surfacing. What right did he have to be happy? How could he laugh and be silly and tell jokes? How could he even smile...ever again?

But he had to. He knew it was time to press forward, to figure out how to get on with his life, and yes, his mother would very much want this for him. He could speculate forever about what might or might not have happened between them. Yet he'd already decided before he even came out to her, that he was done hiding in the closet.

"I think a lot of the questions we have in life are answered on the other side," Dustin said. "The issues she had — the way she struggled with initially accepting you as her gay son — are now resolved. She understands now, don't you think?"

Ivan nodded, wiping his cheek with only his fingertips. He then reached over to the stereo and turned up the volume. Lady Gaga: "Born This Way."

~ ~ ~ ~ ~

Tucker had expected the bar to be hopping on a Friday night, but when he walked in shortly after nine, he could have done a cartwheel down the center aisle and not come close to hitting anyone. He slid onto one of the barstools and was immediately greeted by a smiling, shirtless, college-aged bartender. "Well hello there. What can I get ya?"

Tucker pulled back a bit, straightening his posture in his chair as he gazed at smooth, sunkissed skin that seemed to go on for days. "Um...beer...I guess."

"Name your poison." The blond beamed ear to ear and winked. "Draft beer? Bottled? Corona?"

"Hm. Just a Budweiser."

"Haven't seen you here before." The bartender didn't take his eyes off Tuck as he reached into the cooler for a beer and popped off the cap. "And believe me, I'd remember seeing someone like you." He slipped a napkin on the counter along with the beer. "Want a glass?"

Tucker shook his head. "I thought it would be busier."

"All the creatures of the night are just now waking up. Those bitches gotta have time to get their hair foofed and try on every article of clothing they own. Give it an hour…or two. This place will be packed like a can of sardines." He grinned. "Three fifty."

Tucker pulled out his wallet and handed over a five. "Yeah, I was in here once before, a long time ago. But it was during the week, and there was this guy…"

"You're new to this, aren't ya? Remember the guy's name? I might know him if he's a regular."

"Theo. He was a little older than you, I think. Maybe about my age."

"How old do you think I am?" The bartender stood with one hand on his hip, eyebrows arched slightly.

"Oh, maybe twenty-two."

The young man sighed. "I just turned twenty-one, but I've been serving drinks since I was nineteen. I think I know the dude you're talking about, though. He used to come here all the time, but I haven't seen him in a while. He's kind of a ginger, ain't he?"

"Yeah, sort of reddish-brown hair. Said he worked at a veterinary clinic or something."

"I'm Ben, by the way." He went to hand Tucker his change, but Tucker waved it away. "Thanks." Ben had an adorable smile and a nice, tight physique, but he wasn't the type of guy that excited Tucker. Cute and sexy, but too much a twink.

"I'm Tucker. Nice to meet ya. Yeah, I didn't think the odds were very good I'd see Theo again."

"See what happens when you hook up and don't even bother to exchange numbers? You might be able to find him on Grindr, though. Or if you know his last name…"

"No." Tucker shook his head. "It doesn't matter, and we didn't hook up. Almost, but…"

Ben leaned forward on the bar. "You chickened out?"

"Well, I was sort of…*involved* with someone else at the time."

Ben nodded and reached over to touch Tucker's arm. "A man with integrity. You looked temptation in the face and resisted. I see and hear about so much cheating in this place. It's nice to know there are a few guys left with scruples."

Tucker had to laugh. *Tell that to my ex-wife.* "Well, I'm free now. And alone."

"Trust me, you won't be lonely long, not unless you want to be. A man like you…mmm mmm…stick around a couple minutes and you'll feel like a honeycomb in a beehive. You give 'tall, dark, and handsome' a whole new meaning."

"Thanks. I think." He raised his beer and took a swig. "I got another question for you. You know a guy named Ivan by any chance?"

"You mean the nurse? Ivan Ramsey? Yeah. I know him. I know him real well. *Aaand*…speak of the devil. Ivan!" He raised his hand and waved frantically.

Tucker spun around on his stool and looked over to the entrance. There stood Ivan and another guy, far more flamboyantly dressed, the epitome of every gay stereotype.

"Benjy!" Ivan waved, but was almost immediately distracted by someone from behind, another of his friends who'd just stepped in and greeted him. The bar was already starting to fill up.

"Wow. I guess he's quite popular here."

Ben sighed. "Oh yeah. I think I'm feeling a bit faint. I might need a nurse to come take by blood pressure." Tucker took another swig of his beer. "Or check my temperature rectally." Tucker nearly choked mid-swallow.

Maybe going to the gay bar hadn't been such a good idea after all.

Chapter Six

Every time Ivan hit the gay bar he found himself surrounded by a throng of people who acted as if they were his best friends. He didn't know them, not really. Dustin remained his only out-of-the-closet gay friend, and that was largely due to the fact they were neighbors. But a part of him — perhaps the shallow, self-centered part — relished the attention and affection he soaked up in the gay bar. Eventually, things would change. He saw the middle-aged, single guys standing alone in the corner and wondered if they once enjoyed the warmth of the spotlight. Sadly, so much of the focus within the gay community centered on youth and beauty.

He didn't even remember the name of the person who grabbed him from behind and hugged him, but they acted like he was a long, lost prodigal. Ivan smiled, faking his way across the floor of the bar as Dustin scurried away, glamming it up for his own crowd of groupies.

Weird. When he'd first entered the bar, Benjy the bartender had called out to him. Some guy was sitting next to Benjy at the bar, and strangely enough, he resembled that detective who'd been questioning Ivan. He almost laughed at the absurdity of the comparison. Of course, it had to be someone else. An obviously straight man like Detective Tucker Brown would not be hanging out in a gay club.

As Ivan approached the bar, he casually turned away from the acquaintance he'd been interacting with and glanced down toward the tall, dark, and handsome stranger. And there he was, still sitting with his back to Ivan. He really *did* look a lot like Tucker Brown. Small world. As the barstool began to swivel in Ivan's direction, he realized he was staring, but he caught a glimpse of the man's face before Ivan had a chance to cast his gaze in another direction.

Stunned, Ivan stood still as a statue. It *was* him. It really was Tucker Brown. Mouth agape and eyebrows raised, Ivan shook his head. Benjy had approached on Ivan's side, ready to take his drink order, but Ivan ignored him, stepping closer to the detective. Ivan didn't take his eyes off him as an angry flurry of emotion swept over him.

"What are *you* doing here?" He stopped a couple feet from Tucker's chair.

The detective shrugged and picked up his beer bottle. "Hello, Ivan. I'm having a drink, if you must know. Can I buy you one?"

"No you may *not* buy me a drink, and you can stop stalking me, too!"

Tucker grinned, then took a swig of his beer. He looked Ivan in the eye as he set the bottle back onto the bar. "If I remember correctly, I was here first. Maybe you're the one stalking me."

"Well, well! You found him!" Benjy had stepped over and was directing his comment to Tucker. The bartender turned to Ivan. "What a freaky coincidence. Tucker was just asking about you as you walked through the door."

"Oh really?" Ivan crossed his arms over his chest. "What a small world."

As Ivan glared at the detective, he took pleasure in the way the detective fidgeted momentarily in his seat. And were his cheeks just a shade or two rosier?

"I wasn't stalking you, honest." Tucker sighed. "I was just making small talk with Ben. I knew you were…"

"What? You knew I was what?"

After a pregnant pause, the bartender spoke. "He knew you were thirsty and needed a drink! So what'll it be, Ivy? The usual?"

"Ivy?" Tucker laughed.

"I can buy my own drinks, thank you. And no, the name is *Ivan*, unless you happen to be one of my *friends*. Only they can get away with nicknames."

"Fair enough." Tucker grew serious. "I was just heading out anyway. All of a sudden, it's gotten kind of chilly in here."

Against his better judgment, Ivan took a step forward. The anger within him had nearly reached a boiling point. "You have a lot of nerve. Obviously, you came here tonight to spy on me. I mean, seriously, you don't expect me to buy into the notion that you came here — to a gay bar — for a drink, do you? I know you're straight. I know you have an ex-wife and a child!"

Tucker slid off his stool, now standing inches from Ivan. He stared right into Ivan's eyes, and now he too seemed to be enraged. "You don't know shit about me, and I'll thank you not to make assumptions about things that are none of your damn business."

"When you stalk me like this, you make it my business!" Ivan pointed his finger angrily.

"Get your finger out of my face before I..."

"Before you what?"

"Before I..." Tucker clenched his jaw as his glare intensified. Then suddenly, without warning, he thrust his arms outward and grabbed hold of Ivan, pulling him into himself. Before Ivan knew what was happening, the man's lips smothered his own. Furious, Ivan used both hands to push against the bigger man's chest, but Tucker held firm and delivered the most searing, mind-blowing kiss Ivan had ever experienced. Seconds later, he was surrendering, relaxing his arms as they slid around Tucker's torso. Then instantly, Ivan freaked and pulled back, sputtering.

"You asshole!"

Tucker stood before him smiling as Benjy clapped his hands gleefully. "I'd better make that drink a double!"

~ ~ ~ ~ ~

Of all the stupid, impulsive, fucked-up things Tucker had done in his life, this had to be in the top five. He slammed his palm into the steering wheel. *I kissed him. I fucking kissed him!* Tucker was a police officer, for fuck's sake. Ivan was a person of interest in a criminal investigation Tucker was conducting. Grabbing him like that, forcing himself on the other man — he'd technically committed assault!

There'd surely be hell to pay when this all came out. He'd be taken off the case, reprimanded, possibly even suspended…or worse. And all those co-workers he hadn't yet come out to — well, they'd know now. The whole world would know, and if Ivan made an issue of it and pressed charges, it would surely hit the papers.

He had to tell Janelle. She deserved a warning before she heard it from another source. She was going to be so pissed. If he lost his job, that would impact her and Jaydin. He would lose his insurance coverage, not to mention his income. How would he ever get another police job with something like that on his record? Years of hard work now swirled around the drain ready to be sucked away all because he couldn't keep his fucking hormones in check.

He whipped into Janelle's drive and got out, slamming the door behind him, then headed briskly toward the porch. He stopped abruptly before he reached the first step, then spun around and took a couple steps back toward his car, then turned around again. Suddenly the porch light came on and he stood there staring straight ahead, a deer caught in headlights.

"What'd you do now?" Janelle stood in the threshold, wearing her slippers and bath robe.

"Wh-what makes you think I *did* something."

"It's almost midnight. You're pacing." She ticked off her observations on the fingers of her left hand. "And you have that same guilty look on your face as you did the last time you went to the gay bar."

He hung his head shamefully and sighed.

"Come on, I'll put on a pot of coffee." She motioned him inside.

"Go ahead, say it. I deserve it." He followed her into the kitchen. "I'm pathetic."

"Yes, you *are*." She laughed. "But only because you're acting like Jaydin. For God's sake, Tucker. You're a grown man. You want to tell me what this is all about?"

He slid into one of the kitchen chairs as she slipped a coffee filter into the brewer. "I did go to the gay bar." He looked away, staring at the wall as he spoke. "And...um...I ran into someone."

"And...?"

"And I kind of made a fool of myself and did something really fucking stupid."

She slid the carafe onto the hotplate and laughed. "Oh for fuck's sake, just tell me what you did."

"I kissed Ivan Ramsey!" His head whipped around and he made eye contact with her just as she guffawed.

"Really?" I broad smile spread across her face. "I *knew* you two had some kind of connection."

"We *do!* It's called a criminal investigation, and I just fucking kissed him. Janelle, I've fucked everything up! I could get thrown off the case. I could get suspended, or fired!"

She waved her hand dismissively. "You won't get fired. Briana's not going to let you go over something like that. She might take you off the case, but so what?"Briana Nguyen had been his sergeant since back when he and Janelle were still married. He'd been open with her about the divorce and about his sexual orientation, and she'd been very supportive. She wouldn't support this, though.

"Well, you don't know all the facts." He looked imploringly at his ex-wife.

"All right then." She placed her hands on her hips. "Then just the facts. Spill…"

He took a deep breath. "Ivan…well…he sort of wasn't, ya know…he wasn't expecting it. I sort of, um, *forced* myself on him."

She raised her eyebrows and cocked her head to the side as she surveyed him. She had a way of making him feel about two inches tall when she did that. "And what was his response to this overture?"

"Uh…um…"

"Did he respond to the kiss? Did he kiss you back, surrender to your advances? Or did he pull away, kicking and screaming?"

"Well, both kinda."

She burst into laughter. "Why does that not surprise me? Reminds me of our first kiss."

"Janelle, you're not helping!"

She stepped over to the table and pulled out a chair, then seated herself adjacent him. "He surrendered to your kiss and kissed you back. You didn't assault him, and trust me, he probably wouldn't press charges even if you did."

"But I'm an officer of the law!"

"You're a single gay man with the hots for another single gay man who happens to be drop-dead gorgeous. You kissed him. So what?"

"So *what*? Janelle, this could be the end of my career."

"This is not the end of your career." She placed her hand on his arm. "But it could be the start of something amazing. But you do need to call Briana in the morning, explain what happened. Ask her to reassign the case."

"No, it's not that simple. I can't just walk away from this case. I think I've got it solved."

"So? Turn over the information you've gathered to Viviano...or whoever takes over. What's more important? Getting credit for solving a murder case, or possibly pursuing the love of your life?"

"You don't understand! Janelle, when this case breaks, it's not going to matter who it's assigned to. Ivan Ramsey's going to hate me. He's going to never speak to me again."

"How can you be so sure?"

"Because..." He pushed up out of the chair and stepped over to the counter, then spun around to again face Janelle. "Because I'm about to prove his father is the murderer. Janelle, Ivan's dad killed his wife and is having an affair with another woman!"

~ ~ ~ ~ ~

With the entire day off work, Ivan could sleep as long as he wanted. So why was he lying in his bed wide awake at 7am? He stared up at the ceiling, half convinced he was still asleep and dreaming. The events of the past few weeks seemed more surreal than the visions he had while sleeping. He closed his eyes and immediately remembered Tucker. That man was so fucking annoying, yet Ivan couldn't stop thinking about him.

How dare he make an advance on Ivan like he had the night before! That kind of arrogance and uncalled-for directness infuriated Ivan. The man was so presumptuous, so full of himself. Ivan slid a hand under the covers to find his raging hardon stiff enough to pound nails. He moaned and squeezed his cock, squinting his eyes tightly closed as he remembered the feel of Tucker's rock-solid chest and the smell of his spicy cologne.

It made no sense. Ivan wasn't attracted to men like Tucker. He obviously was a closet case. He'd been married, had a child — an adorable one, at that. How could Ivan ever respect a man who did something so selfish? Yeah, Ivan was all too familiar with the type. Tucker wasn't all that different than Liam. He'd married a woman, probably to use as his beard. He hid behind her skirt while clandestinely fooling around behind her back. What had this done to poor Janelle, his ex-wife? That's probably why they'd gotten divorced in the first place. And what about Jaydin? He deserved a full-time father, a role model he could look up to, not a liar and a cheat like his dad.

"I'll thank you not to make assumptions about things that are none of your damn business."

Was Ivan assuming too much? Was he unfairly projecting his own past experiences onto Tucker? Maybe the situation was nothing like what Ivan imagined. Maybe they had an amicable divorce. Maybe they'd had one of those open relationships Ivan had often heard about but never understood. Maybe Tucker had struggled with some of the same issues while coming out that Ivan himself had endured. It wasn't easy, and had Ivan's mother had her way, he'd have eventually been in the same boat with an ex-wife and God-knows how many kids.

All that aside, Tucker shouldn't have forced himself on Ivan like that. He shouldn't have kissed him without permission. His hand began to glide up and down his smooth, hard shaft. Damn, if Ivan hadn't had the willpower to resist, Tucker would've been sliding his tongue into Ivan's mouth. Ivan gasped and began pumping faster, gripping himself tighter as his pre-cum began to lube his hardon. He threw back the covers and spread his legs, stretching out on the queen-sized mattress. Those lips, he could still feel them against his own and couldn't help but imagine them slippery and wet against his cock. He bucked his hips, thrusting his pelvis up off the mattress.

He was just a cocky, know-it-all cop, and he had no right to violate Ivan the way he had. Oh fuck, he was so close…so damn close. "Violate me!" He moaned as he felt the snap of his cumload being pumped into his shaft—that glorious point of no return! He groaned as his entire body trembled and ropes of cum erupted, splashing against his bare abdomen.

"Shit!" Ivan gasped as he opened his eyes and looked down at the mess he'd made all over himself. He sank back into the plush mattress, allowing the spasms of his abs to abate. His underwear had slid down and were dangling off one ankle. He hadn't even remembered peeling them off but must have done so in his sleep.

He reached over to the bedside stand for tissue when his ringtone went off. *Oh God, please don't let it be work.* He really didn't want to be called in on his weekend off. He fumbled for the phone and picked it up with his non-sticky hand. Brandon.

He used his thumb to accept the call. "Hey, what's up?"

"Ivan, are you up yet?"

"Um...you could say that."

"I need to talk to you. Right away."

He wiped himself with the Kleenex and tossed it into the trash, then pushed himself up onto his side. "What is it? Is something wrong?"

Brandon sighed. "I don't know man. I don't want to say anything over the phone. Can I come over?"

"Yeah, of course."

"Okay, I'll see you in five."

Ivan quickly showered and put on a pot of coffee. He rushed to the door when Brandon arrived, ushering him into the apartment. It wasn't like his brother to act this way. Brandon generally maintained a calm, steady demeanor unfazed by the zingers that life threw at him. He'd been Ivan's rock throughout the funeral, the epitome of strength for their entire family.

Ivan embraced his brother, pulling him close and pressing his head against Brandon's shoulder. Fuck the pretentious bro hugs where you pounded quickly on each other's back or shoulder. Ivan inhaled the scent of his big brother's leather jacket before pulling back. He must've ridden his bike over.

"What's wrong? What happened?"

Brandon looked him in the eye and opened his mouth to speak. Instead, he took a deep breath. "I smell coffee."

"Right. Come in. Black with two sugars, right?"

"Exactly." Brandon followed Ivan into his small kitchen where Ivan poured them each a cup and stirred in his brother's two spoonsful of sugar. He slid the cup across the counter. "You're just like Mom sometimes. I'm a grown man, capable of fixing my own coffee." He smiled at his little brother.

Ivan looked up. "Sorry. Force of habit."

"You don't work today?"

"Just came off my three-day stretch. Got the weekend off."

"Oh, cool. Hopefully you do something fun this weekend." Ivan nodded, not ready to divulge what had happened the night before. Brandon reached inside the front of his jacket and removed a folded piece of paper from his inner pocket. He handed it to Ivan. "Look at this."

Ivan unfolded the letter-sized page and stared at the printout in his hand. "Dad's airline receipt?" He looked back to his brother, confused. "What about it?"

"Look at who's listed as passengers."

"Who's Diane Seavers?"

"Good question." Brandon picked up his coffee mug and took another sip of the steaming java. He managed to do so without slurping, something Ivan couldn't master with hot beverages. "Whoever she is, Dad flew her with him first class."

Ivan shrugged. "Do they even have first class on those domestic flights?"

"Well, business class, but that's not the point. Why is dad taking some other woman to his and mom's vacation condo…less than a month after Mom's death?"

"Hmm." Ivan looked down at the paper in his hand, not sure what to make of it. "Well, I'm sure there's an explanation."

"I'm sure there is too. He's involved with this woman. Ivan, they're having an affair."

Suddenly it felt as if their roles had reversed. Brandon was jumping to conclusions based on very little evidence. This wasn't like him. He usually was so measured, so rational. "Well, maybe she's a business associate."

"The whole point of the trip was to get away from everything, to vacation."

Ivan handed back the receipt and picked up his own coffee, slurping it noisily. "Why don't we just wait and ask him when he comes home? She's probably a friend, maybe someone Dad did business with. He probably didn't tell us about her because…well, because of *this*. He probably figured we'd get the wrong idea and freak out."

Brandon sighed dramatically. "You don't understand. There's more."

"What do you mean, there's more?" For the first time in years, Brandon was beginning to annoy him. Ivan didn't need any of this right now. None of them did. The family needed to stick together rather than turn on each other and question every move the others made. "Look, no offense, but I don't care. You know how close I was to Mom. I loved her…more than anything. But they say when a married couple is truly happy, they usually do remarry rather quickly after one of them is widowed. Dad's not a loner. He's not strong enough. Look at how much he relied on Mom, and maybe…well, maybe this other woman is the friend he needs right now."

"He quadrupled Mom's life insurance two months ago."

Shocked, Ivan stared at his big brother. He held out both hands and shrugged. "So?"

"You don't find that odd? Why would Dad all of a sudden do that? Not only is he getting the money for the house which burnt to the ground, but he's also getting half a million for Mom's death!"

Ivan felt his jaw clenching along with his fists. "You know what? You're being ridiculous. Dad has always been a businessman. I'm sure over the years he and Mom routinely assessed their insurance needs and made adjustments. That's what normal people do. Mom's dead! No amount of money can make up for that, and I'm sure Dad will be the first person to say that. Of course, he'd trade all the money in the world for one more day…"

The crestfallen look on Brandon's face stopped Ivan before he could finish the sentence. "I know all this is hard to believe, and I'm sorry." He stepped closer to Ivan, then placed a hand on his younger brother's shoulder. "I have copies of his credit card statement."

"You *what*? Brandon, how could you?"

"The day Mom died, he made a fifteen thousand dollar purchase at a jewelers. And he spent a couple hundred bucks at Home Depot."

"So he was buying Mom a ring. And so what, he went to Home Depot. Shopping for hardware is his Goddamn hobby. He sold it his whole life and has every imaginable tool known to mankind."

"Ivan, please."

"No! This is ridiculous, Brandon. I can't believe I'm hearing these words come out of *your* mouth. You're all but accusing our own father of…I can't even fucking say it!"

"Where is the ring? Why didn't he mention it to us? Why didn't he show us the ring or have Mom buried with it?"

"I don't know! I don't fucking know!" Ivan turned away, running both hands through his hair. Confused and frustrated, he doubled over, then took a deep breath before righting himself. He spun back around to face his brother. "Maybe it was too painful. Have you ever thought of that? Maybe he's saved the ring and is keeping it as a memento."

"Let's call him. Let's just call and ask him, okay?"

"So that he knows you've been going behind his back spying on him? So that he thinks we suspect he murdered our mother? Are you fucking crazy?"

The stern expression on Brandon's face gradually softened, and as he gazed into Ivan's eyes it wasn't anger that Ivan sensed. It was worse than that. Brandon pitied him, and that enraged Ivan. How dare he jump to these outlandish conclusions and then have the nerve to feel sorry for Ivan because he didn't concur?

"I want you to leave." Ivan glared into his Brandon's eyes. "Now."

"Ivan, please."

"Just go. I've heard enough. You do realize Mom's death was a murder, and there's an open investigation. These crazy allegations don't help matters. Our entire family is already under the microscope. What do you think that detective would say about all this? He'd probably come arrest our father—the only parent we have left!"

"You think I haven't thought of all this? Ivan—"

"Get out! Get the fuck out of my home!"

Brandon held up both hands, palms outward. "Okay, okay. I'm going to leave. But please...please call me when you calm down."

"Don't hold your breath. I will *never* calm down enough to accept our dad is a murderer, that he killed our mother. Never!"

Brandon stuffed the receipt back into his pocket and turned toward the door. He took a couple steps then turned his head to look back at Ivan. "I love you. No matter what." And he left.

Chapter Seven

Tucker really needed to hire a housekeeper. Dishes cluttered the kitchen countertops, left from two days prior when he'd made supper for Jaydin and him. He had laundry piling up, vacuuming to get done, and a whole hell of a lot of clutter to get rid of. Had he actually let Janelle do most of the housework when they were together? She used to say as much, but he never really saw the evidence until now. If he didn't have someone around to pick up after him, he had a tendency to just let things go.

Well, maybe his obsession with his caseload had something to do with it. And the facts he'd uncovered while investigating the Ramsey case were staggering. Maybe it was a good thing he was going to be taken off the case. He wasn't sure how he'd face Ivan. Tucker didn't relish the idea of the young man finding out his own father had killed Ivan's mother. Tucker couldn't imagine what it would be like to first lose one parent and then have the other whisked away to prison for the rest of their life.

And of all the goddamned, stupid-ass things for him to do, why'd he have to haul off and kiss Ivan like he'd done the night before? That really made a mess of everything. He needed to take Janelle's advice and call his boss, ask her to reassign the case. He sat in his recliner, staring at his phone. She might not appreciate a call so early in the morning. It was Saturday, after all, and only a little after eight o'clock.

He snatched the phone off the stand and held it in his hand, heaving a defeated sigh. Before he could pull up his boss' number, his ringtone sounded. He stared down at the number, trying to recall why it looked familiar. No, it couldn't be. Why on earth was Ivan calling him again and at such an early hour? Fuck, it had to be about the damn kiss.

He pressed the button and held the phone to his ear. "Hello. Detective Brown." The line seemed dead at first. No one responded. "Hello? Ivan?"

"Detective…" Ivan's voice was strained, an octave or two higher than the normal timbre. "I need to talk to you."

"If this is about last night…"

"It's not about that. Although…well, we should probably talk about that too, but it's about my dad and my brother. I didn't…uh…I didn't know who else to call. I think my dad…"

Tucker pushed himself up in the chair, straightening his posture. "Ivan, you realize I'm investigating this case. Maybe you should be calling an attorney."

"You probably already know, things don't look good right now. If you've discovered the evidence my brother showed me this morning…"

"Which is why you shouldn't be talking to me…and why I shouldn't be talking to *you*."

"You fucking kissed me, for God's sake! You can at least—"

Fuck! He was about to lose it. Ivan was about to start crying over the phone. "It's okay. Wait. I know how upset you must be, how hurt."

"You have no fucking idea." Now he really was crying. *Son of a bitch.* "There has to be some other explanation. There's no way my dad would betray my mother like this. Even if it's true he's been having an affair, I can't believe he'd *kill* my mom!"

"Ivan, listen to me. The truth is going to come out, and you might be right. What I want you to know is that if he's innocent, we'll figure it out. We aren't going to charge someone with a crime unless we know with certainty."

"I want to…"

"What?"

"I want to see you. I want to talk to you about what you know."

"Ivan, no. I can't do that. I can't discuss this case with you or anyone. I'm sure you understand the importance of confidentiality."

"Then I want to see you about…" The phone went silent again for a few seconds. "I want to talk to you about last night."

"That was a mistake, and I'm sorry. I shouldn't have been so pushy, and…and…and it was just completely inappropriate."

"You almost made me come in my fucking pants. Tucker…can I call you Tucker? I can't stop thinking about it."

Was this for real? Was Ivan as conflicted about his feelings as Tucker was, or was this just a ruse? He could just be playing Tucker, feigning interest in order to get what he wanted — information about the case.

"I know what you're thinking," Ivan went on. "You think I'm just trying to get close to you because of the case."

Tucker coughed, holding one hand over the phone. "I don't know what to think. What about the things you said to me last night? You didn't seem all that interested in me then."

"Oh really? Will you do something for me Tucker? Please…"

"What?"

"Close your eyes."

"Huh?"

"Close your fucking eyes. Forget about anything we said to each other. Just close your eyes and remember the kiss."

Before closing them, Tucker rolled his eyes, annoyed. But he did as Ivan requested and closed his eyes, sinking back a bit in his chair as he did so. He thought about that moment, about how angry and sexy and down-right gorgeous Ivan was as he stood there waving his finger in Tucker's face. And he remembered the impulse, the sudden urge that had overtaken him. He reached out and grabbed hold of Ivan's shoulders and pulled him in, and...oh fucking God! He responded. His whole damned body responded as he seemed to just melt into Tucker's embrace. The feel of him, his scent, the taste of his mouth! He remembered it all and as his eyes shot open he realized he was groping himself.

"Meet me at the diner on the corner of Williams Road in half an hour. We're going on a road trip." Tucker said the words without bothering to think through his actions. He couldn't walk away from this guy. He couldn't drop the case and forget he'd ever met Ivan Ramsey, so instead he went all in — head first.

~ ~ ~ ~ ~

The last time Ivan ate at this restaurant was with his brother and father, the day he found out his mom's death had not been accidental. A nosey reporter had come over to their table asking intrusive questions. Ivan looked around, fearing a repeat of the incident. He didn't want to be seen dining with the detective, especially not by a reporter.

He spotted Tucker Brown in a corner booth nursing a cup of coffee. Ivan stopped in his tracks, staring for a moment. Maybe this was a mistake after all. Why would this man have any motivation to help Ivan or his family? Tucker's job was to solve crimes and to convict criminals. He was seeking evidence to build a case against Ivan's father, and it made zero sense for Ivan to even associate with the man.

He took a deep breath, steeling himself, and commenced. Determined to appear confident, he slid into the booth and looked Tucker in the eye as the detective surmised him. The man's mere presence exuded strength and self-assuredness. He was a cop, after all, and didn't all police officers view the law as a set of absolutes? Expecting empathy and compassion from a man like this was like expecting a lion to feel sorry for the zebra it was about to eat.

Butterflies fluttered in Ivan's stomach as he opened his mouth to speak. Words didn't immediately come out, so he just sat there a few seconds gaping like a fish out of water. "Um, thanks for agreeing to…um…see me. You said you wanted me to take a road trip with you?"

Before Tucker could respond, a waitress appeared with a carafe of coffee. Ivan informed her he'd not be ordering food and commenced to open three creamer cups and stir them into his beverage. Tucker just sat there watching, still silent. At last, Ivan looked up, and their gazes locked on each other.

"I'm only like a hundred percent sure this is a terrible idea," Tucker said, glowering. "I think the best thing I could do at this point would be to resign from the case. I'm thinking of calling my sergeant and requesting she take me off it."

"No, wait…" Ivan bit his bottom lip as he stared imploringly at the broad-shouldered detective. "I don't want you to do that."

"Why?"

"I don't know." He sighed, then looked down at the coffee he was still stirring. "I'm not sure what to think anymore, but I need to know the truth about what happened."

"Really? And what if the truth is uglier than you could ever imagine?"

"My mother was murdered." He again looked up at Tucker. "It doesn't get any uglier than that, does it?"

Tucker raised his eyebrows. "I'm afraid it might." He spoke softly, barely whispering. "I know your father had a motive for killing your mother. I know he potentially had a weapon and a means." He stopped talking long enough to breathe. "And I know he was having an affair, but what I don't know is how to explain his alibi."

"Can't you just confirm that he was where he claimed to be, at a motel in Deckerville?"

Tucker nodded. "Of course, and I've already done that. He checked into the motel at 4:43pm on Thursday, the night before the murder. He also used his credit card that day at Home Depot in Deckerville, and he ordered takeout Chinese that was delivered to his room that evening."

"And?"

"And he was still checked in at the hotel the next morning when the police contacted him by cell phone. He checked out, drove back to Fulton, and was first seen by the police around ten-thirty."

"Right around the time I saw him."

"Correct. He was contacted by phone, and an officer went to your brother's home. Your brother then went directly to the hospital where you were just finishing your shift."

Ivan took a sip of his coffee. "I don't get it. Then what's this road trip all about?"

"Deckerville is approximately two hours and thirty-seven minutes from Fulton. He ordered his takeout food at 11:47pm."

"What? Why would they be open so late?"

"Twenty-four hour delivery. It's in their Internet ad. Guaranteed thirty-minute delivery."

"So Dad had a late-night craving for rice and vegetables, I still don't see your point. How could he have committed the murder when he was in an entirely different place? You don't think he hired someone to do it, do you?"

Tucker shook his head. "I don't see any evidence of that, but I also don't see this as an airtight alibi. The desk clerk at the hotel confirms that your father called the front desk just before 1am to request a 9am wake-up call."

"That is so like my dad. He knew nothing about using his own Smartphone. Would've been easier to just set his phone alarm."

"Right, but by requesting the wakeup call from his room phone, he has further solidified his alibi. That doesn't leave much of a window for him to drive all the way to Fulton and back before morning. I want to drive there myself and time it precisely. And I want to check their surveillance videos for clues to either prove or disprove the alibi."

Ivan leaned forward. This whole thing seemed bizarre, something straight out of an episode of Forensic Files. "Since when do motels have surveillance cameras?"

"They have a couple outside cameras of their parking lot and entrance, and they have one in their lobby."

"Good! Then we'll know for sure if my dad left that evening. If he didn't, then he's free and clear."

Tucker nodded. "And if he did..."

"Well, come on then. Let's get going. Why're we wasting time here drinking coffee."

"Oh, I don't know. I thought maybe it was just a matter of you enjoying my company."

"*You* can enjoy *my* company in the car. You're driving, right?"

"Of course." Tucker pulled out his wallet and threw some currency on the table. "Let's hit the road then."

Chapter Eight

By inviting Ivan to ride with him, Tucker had essentially locked himself into a tiny cubicle with the young nurse for a five-plus hour time span. It hadn't been the most thought-out suggestion he'd ever made, and as they drove out of Fulton, Tucker was already regretting his decision.

Ivan stared out the passenger window, not even glancing in Tucker's direction, and Tucker wasn't sure how to interpret his silence. He gulped a couple times before finally deciding to bite the bullet and address the obvious elephant in the room—or the car, perhaps.

"I just wanted to say, I'm sorry about last night. I don't know what got into me at the bar. I had no right to grab you like that and—"

"Practically force your tongue down my throat."

Tucker shook his head slightly, not taking his eyes off the road. "You didn't open your mouth. How could I?"

"See!" Ivan turned his head quickly to face Tucker. "You admit it. That's what you were trying to do, and you would have if I'd have let you."

Tucker couldn't help himself. He smiled just a little which didn't seem at all to please Ivan who again looked away from him. "Well, it must've been memorable to you," Tucker said. "You're the one who asked me to close my eyes and think about it when we were on this phone earlier. And you said you almost came in your pants."

"So?"

Tucker wanted to reach across the seat and touch him, but everything about Ivan's body language told him he shouldn't.

Ivan leaned against his door, head resting against the window pane. Was he grieving over his mother and thinking about the horror that his own father might have murdered her? Or was he angry? Was he truly pissed at Tucker for coming onto him the night before. Fuck, it really sucked not knowing how to interpret Ivan's signals.

"So it turned you on, but you're still pissed at me?"

"Oh for God's sake! Is it so hard to understand I just might have other things on my mind besides you and your damn kiss? I threw Brandon out of my apartment this morning. He'll probably never speak to me again."

"I'm sorry." Tucker meant it. Seeing Ivan this way in so much pain wasn't easy. Had Tucker been in the same situation, he'd likely have done the exact same thing. Of course, Ivan's natural reaction would be to defend his father. "I don't know Brandon all that well, but from what I've learned of him, he seems like a very reasonable person. I'm sure he'll understand you were just upset and will forgive you."

"Sometimes I just think he's *too* reasonable." Ivan shifted in his seat, inching closer to Tucker, then turned his head to look at him. "I don't even know how to describe how I'm feeling. Everything is so foggy right now, like I'm not living in the real world. All this shit is so crazy. There's this knot in my chest that doesn't go away. It's like a lump right here." He pointed his finger toward his sternum. "I try to swallow it, and it won't go down. I try to get on with my life, think of things to make myself happy..."

"You're grieving. Ivan, your mom just died. It's going to take more than a month to get over it. You might *never* get over it completely."

"The twisted thing is that I don't really want to. I'm afraid if I stop hurting, that'll mean I've let go of her memory, and she'll be gone forever." Tears streamed down his cheeks. Tucker finally reached over and slid his hand into Ivan's, squeezing it gently.

"I haven't lost a parent, but my older brother was killed in a car accident when he was only seventeen."

"Oh fuck. That must've been awful." Ivan continued to hold Tucker's hand.

"I get why you're upset about Brandon. You've both lost your mom, and maybe even your dad. You can't let this destroy the relationship you have with each other."

"I was just so angry, ya know. All I could think about at the time was that he was showing me this shit about our dad. It was like he was the enemy somehow. It's crazy, I know."

"He was the bearer of bad news, but I have a feeling he's smart enough to figure out you were reacting to the news itself — not him."

"You think so? I said some pretty mean things to him."

"Did he say mean shit back to you?"

Ivan shook his head. "No," he whispered. "He said to call him when I calmed down."

Tucker glanced over to him. "Call."

Ivan took a deep breath, then released Tucker's hand. He reached into his pocket and pulled out his phone. "Should I tell him I'm with you?"

Tucker gripped the steering wheel a little tighter. "It's up to you, but I'd rather you didn't. I haven't figured out yet how exactly I'm going to explain this to my partner...or my boss. There's no logical reason why you're sitting in this car beside me.

Ivan smiled. "I should be the one saying that. You're trying to arrest my father. You're a damn cop, for God's sake. And you're a divorced closet case. There's not a single thing about you I normally find attractive."

"Really? Not even one?"

Ivan looked down at his phone, ignoring the question. He scrolled to his brother's number and dialed. "Brandon, I'm so sorry. Will you forgive me?"

"Two hours and twenty-three minutes." Ivan looked down at his phone as they pulled into the motel entrance.

"The trip is likely to be even shorter in the middle of the night. We had traffic to contend with and a line at the toll booth." Tucker cringed internally as he looked over at Ivan. The pain was written all over Ivan's face. That guy wore his feelings like a billboard.

"Well, it's no surprise." Ivan sighed. "We already pretty much knew how long it would take. The distance itself doesn't prove anything, and it certainly doesn't discount my father's alibi."

Tucker nodded. "I've got to go inside and get a copy of the surveillance video. They're supposed to have it ready for me at the desk."

"Fine." Ivan unfastened his seat belt, then reached for his door handle.

"Wait." Tucker reached over, placing a hand against Ivan's arm. "I should probably go alone."

Ivan glared at him. "I don't *think* so. It was my mom who was murdered. I have a right…"

"Ivan, please…"

"How the fuck is the motel clerk going to know I'm not your partner?"

"They have a right to ask for I.D. and it's standard procedure to show our badges."

"You show your badge then. I'll take my chances, but I didn't ride over here just to wait in the car. I have a few questions I need answered."

"Ivan, no!" Before Tucker could stop him, Ivan shot out of his seat and was heading across the parking lot toward the motel lobby. Fuck, why'd he have to be damned bull-headed? Tucker pushed open his door and jumped out of his seat, slamming his door behind him. He raced to catch up and finally grabbed hold of Ivan's arm. "You can't be asking questions."

"The fuck I can't! This is *my* family. *My* mom was killed, and I have a right to know. How long was he coming here? Was he with that other woman—that Diane or Diana, whoever the fuck she was? Did he leave anything behind in the room, anything that might be a clue...?"

"Do you fucking think I haven't already asked all those questions? Jesus Christ! If there's anything you want to know, just ask me, but don't go in there all half-cocked, shooting your mouth off. If you do, someone's going to complain, and I'll get kicked off the case...or worse."

"That's all you care about, isn't it?" Ivan pulled away from him, stepping backward a couple of paces. "You think only of yourself and your precious job."

"No, that's not true!" Damn, he was so fucking infuriating. Why the hell didn't he listen? Why couldn't Ivan just *try* to understand? "If this case is compromised in any way—if the defense can even suggest that the evidence-gathering process was contaminated or somehow improper—the murderer could get off on a technicality!"

"My dad, you mean!"

"Whoever it is. Look, you've got to calm down." He stepped forward and grabbed hold of Ivan's shoulders. "Please, can you just trust me? I know how to do my job. And no, this job is not the only thing I care about." He pulled Ivan closer to him. "I can't imagine what you've gone through." Ivan's arms snaked around his torso. Tucker squeezed him tighter, pressing Ivan's head against his shoulder. He spoke quietly, whispering into Ivan's ear. "Just let me go in and get the CD. I'll only be a minute, and then we can go back and watch it together."

"What if this proves my dad is guilty?"

"We'll go where the facts lead us…even if it's hard. And I'll be there with you. I promise."

Ivan pulled back and looked up into Tucker's eyes. "But you hardly know me."

Tucker felt the corners of his lips curl as he gazed into the sweet, unassuming face. "I know this sounds crazy, but it doesn't feel like we're strangers. I feel like I've known you forever."

"I don't know why either, but I feel it too…as annoying and bossy as you are. It doesn't make sense."

"Me? You say *I'm* the bossy one?" Tucker laughed. "You should listen to yourself sometime."

Ivan scowled defiantly, hands on both hips. "I'm not bossy, but I'm also not the submissive type. I'm not about to let you or anyone else order me around. It's only because you're used to strutting around all Alpha-Male that you think anyone who has the balls to defy you is annoying."

Tucker shook his head and sighed. "And we were finally starting to bond."

"I'll wait in the car. But hurry up!" He turned and headed back to the sedan.

"Yes *sir*!" Tucker shouted and saluted.

Ivan, without turning around, saluted back. He used only one finger.

~ ~ ~ ~ ~

"I'm not sure if I'm even ready to find out." Ivan was back to looking out the window. He vacillated in his mind, one second just wanting to know the truth, wanting to find out quickly — get it over with like ripping off a Band Aid. The next second, he wanted to recoil into himself and pretend none of this had happened. "The day Mom died, I wanted to just crawl in bed and pretend it had all been a bad dream. I wanted to wake up and discover I'd had a nightmare."

"You don't have to watch the video with me." Tucker had turned off the main road, and Ivan had no idea where they were heading.

"Where are we going?"

"Thought I'd stop and get us some lunch."

Ivan wrapped one arm around his stomach. He really was hungry, but he didn't know if he could eat. "You just passed a Panera back there."

Tucker made a face, and Ivan almost laughed. "Panera? What the fuck? That shit's rabbit food."

"Let me guess, you're taking us for greasy burgers, right?"

The sly grin on Tucker's face followed by a moment of silence told Ivan he was right.

"No, not greasy, really. Well...sort of. It's just that Deckerville has one of the last remaining A & W drive-in restaurants in the state. I thought maybe a good ole fashioned root beer float might cheer you up a bit."

"Oh God, I haven't been to an A & W in ages. I used to beg Mom for the Papa Burger basket, but she only ever let me get the Baby Burger."

"Ha! And you're preaching to me about grease."

"Well, I didn't know anything about clogged arteries and heart attacks back then." Ivan had shifted in his seat and was now facing Tucker. He glanced down at Tucker's lap, taking in the sight of his long legs. The fabric of his Chinos stretched tight around his crotch. "And maybe she didn't think I was ready to handle such a big piece of meat."

"Well, I'll get you a Papa Burger today then. I'm guessing you'll handle it just fine."

As Tucker pulled into the restaurant and parked under the drive-in awning, Ivan was blasted into the past. As a kid he'd loved the uniqueness of the drive-in experience, placing the orders through the speaker menu and having them delivered on a tray that hung on the car window.

"Want to eat in the car, or over at one of the picnic tables?" Tucker turned to him as he spoke, his voice lilting slightly.

"You bring Jaydin here, don't you?"

Growing a bit more serious, Tucker straightened his posture. "Um...why?"

"You're talking to me like I'm a four year old."

"Oh. Sorry."

"Force of habit?" Ivan smiled. "Believe me, I understand. I spend hours talking to little kids every day. I sometimes forget how to grown-up."

"Well, please don't tell his mom. She doesn't approve of fast food, but Jaydin's favorite thing on earth is ice cream. Well...that and Star Wars."

"Don't worry, your secret's safe with me. Let's get a picnic table."

"Okay, let me place the order." He pressed the call button on the speaker menu. "You want the Papa burger basket and a root beer float?"

"With diet root beer."

"What?" Tucker offered a look of incredulity. "That's sacrilegious. "

"And pointless, I know." Ivan shrugged. "But I only drink diet soda. I can't stand the taste of sugar-sweetened pop."

"And, of course, that ice cream has no sugar in it."

"Are you gonna order me the float or argue? I don't care if it makes sense to you. That's what I like."

Tucker raised his hands in surrender. "Fine, fine. A diet root beer float."

"Thank you."

"Welcome to A & W. May I take your order?" The voice through the speaker sounded scratchy and mechanical, adding to the retro ambiance. Tucker placed their order, informing the attendant they'd be dining at one of the picnic tables. Ivan reached for his door handle and pushed it open, stepping out of the car. His mouth was already watering in anticipation of the burger.

Tucker walked around the front of the car and led the way over to the side of the building where a group of tables had been arranged. Each table had its own umbrella. Ivan followed, staring down at the perfectly rounded globes of the detective's ass. Those pants really did fit him like a glove. *Speaking of mouth-watering.*

As they sat across from each other, Tucker looked into Ivan's eyes. "I hate to beat a dead horse. We probably don't need to keep talking about last night, but there's one more thing I wanted to say."

"Okay…"

"I've apologized for what I did." He looked down at the table in front of him and then raised his head to reestablish eye contact. "But that's not a hundred percent honest. I'm sorry I was so forward, but I don't regret the kiss."

Ivan felt his cheeks warming. "I'm not sure why, but…" He took a deep breath. "But I don't regret it either."

"Even though there's not a single thing about me you find attractive?"

"I never said that. I said none of your characteristics are the things I usually find attractive in a man. You defy my 'type'." He raised both hands to make air quotes.

The waitress arrived with the root beer floats. Both were served in hefty glass mugs, and they were filled to the brim, a huge swirl of whipped cream extending three inches above the rim.

"Holy Moses!" Ivan exclaimed, then laughed. "I forgot how big these are."

He thanked the waitress and then picked up the straw, unwrapping it. He slid one end into the drink and placed his lips around the other as he looked across the table at Tucker who was now staring at him intently. Puckering his lips, Ivan sucked.

Tucker bit his bottom lip and leaned back a bit on the bench. "Uh, how is it?"

"Mmm, creamy." Ivan raised his eyebrows.

"So what exactly is your type then?"

Ivan leaned back and picked up the long plastic spoon. "Let's just say I don't have a lot of respect for gay guys who act like they're ashamed of who they are. I think it's really shitty for a gay man to marry a woman when he knows he's not really attracted to her."

Tucker, who hadn't yet touched his float, picked up his own spoon and scooped up a dollop of whipped cream. He slid it into his mouth. "And that's what you think I did?"

"Didn't you?"

Tucker offered sort of a half-shrug. "Well, technically, I guess. But even though I knew at the time I got married that I was attracted to guys, I was still in denial. I didn't ask Janelle to marry me so that I could hide my sexuality, though. I married her because I loved her."

"So you're saying that you're bi?"

"I'm not saying anything of the sort." He plunged into his float with the spoon, digging deeper in order to claim some of the vanilla ice cream. "Although, if I were bisexual, what would be wrong with that?"

"Nothing, I guess." It seemed bisexuality was a terminology a lot of closeted gay men used to explain away their fear of discovery.

"Whether you understand it or not, a lot of people truly are bisexual. You're the educated one. You should know this already. Sexual orientation is a continuum. You know—the Kinsey Scale?"

Ivan sighed. "If you're not bisexual, why were you attracted to Janelle, and in love with her?"

"I was attracted to the person. She's my best friend, but even after we were married I always felt guilty that I didn't feel the attraction to her physically that I thought I should. But that never made me love her any less. And divorcing her—fuck, that was the hardest thing I've ever done. I think I took it harder than she did."

Was he being dismissive of his ex-wife's feelings...or simply honest? "She knows about you now then?"

"She's the one who initiated the conversation. She more or less forced me to admit who I am and come out of the closet. That was two years ago, and since then I've come out to my folks and most of my coworkers."

"Really? What about Jaydin?"

"Jaydin's four. We aren't hiding anything from him, but the sexual orientation topic hasn't really come up yet. I suppose when I meet someone and start seriously dating, I'll have to have a conversation with him."

He sounded so sincere. Perhaps Ivan had misjudged him. He'd been projecting a lot of what he felt about Liam onto Tucker. "I was in a relationship once with a guy who wanted to remain in the closet. His plan was to marry a woman and see me on the side."

"I hope you kicked his ass to the curb."

Ivan tried to swallow, but the lump in his throat wouldn't immediately go down. "He was my first. I was crazy about him. We were a couple for two and a half years."

The empathy in Tucker's eyes seemed to betray his identity as a hard-core, just-the-facts detective. "I sometimes beat myself up about the choices I made. I know I didn't exactly make things easy for Janelle, even though I never intended to hurt her. Still, looking back, how can I now say I'd do anything differently? If so, I wouldn't have Jaydin, and...well, really, he's all that matters to me. Or he's the one who matters the most, ya know."

Ivan did know. He understood completely, and as a pediatric nurse he'd witnessed firsthand the strength of this parental bond. No matter what he ultimately thought of Tucker, Ivan would always respect the relationship the man had with his son.

"You're a really good dad." He meant the compliment. He'd seen Tucker with Jaydin.

"Thank you."

The waitress arrived with a tray of burgers and fries, and Ivan stared down at the fast food delight in front of him. "You track down murderers for a living, but look at this. You're trying to kill me."

"Death by a thousand cuts."

"No." Ivan grinned. "Death by a thousand bites of yumminess." He snatched a fry and tossed it into his mouth. "Now let's see if I can get my mouth around this big piece of meat."

Chapter Nine

Had Ivan actually gone for two full hours without thinking about his mother's death? As Tucker pulled his car into the driveway, reality struck. Ivan grew serious, remembering why he was with the handsome detective. For most of the ride back from Deckerville, they'd laughed and talked. Tucker had reached across the seat a couple of times to touch Ivan's arm. It was nice to be thinking of something other than the harsh reality Ivan now faced.

"You sure you want to go through with this? I can drive you back to the diner to pick up your car."

"No, I really want to see the video. I *need* to."

"And what if it destroys your father's alibi?"

Ivan looked down at the dashboard, not wanting to make eye contact in the moment. "I don't know. I'll have to accept it for what it is. Either way, I already know Dad hadn't been faithful to my mom. Not only was he cheating on her, but he's already moved on."

Ivan closed his eyes as he felt Tucker's hand on his shoulder. "We don't know that for sure."

"Jesus, Tucker. He bought her a fucking diamond."

"Or he bought it for your mother…"

"And then secretly flew to Florida with this other woman? And why wouldn't he have bothered to even mention the ring to Brandon or me?" Ivan turned to look at Tucker. "It is what it is. I already know he was cheating, and you know what? I just hope Mom didn't know. I hope she hadn't found out. I'd hate to think about how much it would have hurt her."

"Let's just go look at the video then. We only have to view the camera at the exit from 1am on. If your father's car never left the property during that time period, his alibi is air tight. We know already that he had checked into the motel and that he ordered a wakeup call from his room."

Ivan nodded. "And what do we do if he does have a solid alibi?"

"*We* don't do anything. It's not your job to solve this murder."

Clenching his fists, Ivan glowered at Tucker. "I *want* to solve it. I need to know what happened!"

"Or maybe you need to focus on your family and leave the police work to me." He squeezed Ivan's shoulder. "Please…"

"Let's just go watch the fucking video." Ivan pulled away, pushing the door open to free himself from the car.

~ ~ ~ ~ ~

Tucker should have spent a few more minutes cleaning his house. He scanned the room as they stepped across the threshold of the entryway into the kitchen. "Uh, sorry about the mess."

"Not much of a housekeeper, huh?"

"Guess I just don't think about it. I have a tendency to let things go, and then suddenly I remember I'm going to have to go pick up Jaydin and bring him back to this pigsty. Then I at least try to tidy up a bit."

Ivan laughed. "With your fat law enforcement salary, you should be able to afford a maid."

"And you should get off whatever drugs you're on." Tucker grinned as he stepped over to the fridge. "Want a beer?"

"If you have water…"

"Of course, I have water." He pulled open the refrigerator door and retrieved two bottled waters from the lower shelf. "And I have cherry Kool Aid, Jaydin's favorite. Bug Juice. Chocolate milk."

"Forget the maid. You need to hire yourself a nutritionist. What're you doing giving Jaydin all that crap?"

"Crap?" Tucker extended his arm, handing Ivan one of the waters. "What's wrong with Kool Aid?"

"Hm. Well, no nutritional value, loaded with sugar…"

"I buy the sugar-free."

"I think you can't resist spoiling him. You cave in and give him what he wants…like greasy cheeseburgers, ice cream, and root beer floats."

Tucker stared at him a moment, amused. "Who's the detective here? Am I under investigation for child endangerment?"

"I should have you two over some night to my apartment. I know a lot of foods kids love that are also healthy. I could teach you."

"Or you could come here? I have this great big kitchen…"

"Hire the maid first, and then we'll talk."

Tucker shook his head, sighing. Had Ivan just kinda-sorta invited him on a date, or had he insulted Tucker? Or both? "You're definitely a better cook than me. I'm good on the grill, and that's about it."

Ivan unscrewed the cap of his water and took a swig. "And let me guess, you make the world's best pancakes?"

"You've been talking to Jaydin."

"No." Ivan shook his head. "I just know your type."

"Wait a second, you're stereotyping me." He took a step closer.

"You're a walking stereotype. Sorry, man, but you put a capital T in testosterone. You probably also love football and action movies. And you've probably never picked up a fictional novel in your life, at least not any with literary value."

Tucker stood there for a few seconds just glaring. *What a fucking crock of bullshit assumptions!* "Come here!" He grabbed Ivan's elbow and marched him across the kitchen into the living room. "How dare you try to put me in that kind of box! You know nothing about me." He pointed to the far wall of the living room where a huge twelve-foot bookshelf resided.

"Holy Moses." Ivan pulled away from Tucker and walked over to the book case. "I'd have never guessed."

"Big surprise! I'm smart enough to read."

"And not just pop-up books." Ivan removed one of the books from Tucker's shelf of classics. "I'd have never suspected you to be a fan of English literature. I read this book back in high school." He held up the copy of *Great Expectations*.

"I generally prefer contemporary, but I'll read anything."

"Really?"

"Mysteries are my favorite."

Ivan turned back around to re-shelve the book, then found the section of Tom Clancy novels. "I'll be damned." He looked back at Tucker and smiled.

"Well?"

"Well, what?"

"Well…" Tucker crossed his arms across his chest. "Are you going to apologize?"

Ivan laughed and offered the most incredulous look of bewilderment. "Huh?"

"Twice now you've admitted to judging me, making assumptions about who I am."

"Twice?" Ivan mimicked Tucker's posture, crossing his own arms obstinately. "Who's the one on drugs?"

"Earlier you said you thought I was a closet case who selfishly married a woman to hide my true identity. And now you're admitting that you thought I was a moron who never reads."

"I didn't say either of those things!"

"Yeah, you did...in other words. But you said them. You totally judged me, dude."

"I...I..." Ivan raised both hands in the air, shaking his head emphatically. "You know what? I don't *care*. I don't give a flying fuck what you're like, because it's none of my business."

"And yet you can't help yourself. You *make* it your business. You look down on me, don't you?"

"No!" Ivan took a step closer to him. "I don't look down on anyone."

"You think with your college degree and upper-middle-class fancy houses and timeshares in Florida, and fifteen thousand dollar diamonds, that you're better than a know-nothing beat cop who happened to get a lucky promotion to detective."

"Fuck you! I'm not like that, and that shit you just said... that's not me at all. That's my parents! You know, my dead mother and my father who probably killed her!"

"You know I didn't mean —"

"Tucker, you're such an —"

"You're infuriating!"

"You're so Goddamn cocky!" Ivan took another step closer.

"You're such a know-it-all!" Tucker advanced a few inches further in Ivan's direction, his heart beating like a bongo.

"You never listen!" Ivan reached out, grabbing hold of Tucker's shoulders.

"You're...you're...you're...!" Tucker stared into shorter man's eyes.

"Going to fucking kiss you!" Ivan thrust himself forward, on tip-toe, and mashed his mouth forcefully against Tucker's. Tucker pulled him in, responding to the kiss as he tilted his head to the side. Within seconds their hands were all over each other, Ivan caressing Tucker's shoulders as Tucker found Ivan's waist and lifted him inches off the ground. They kissed passionately and deeply, exploring each other's mouth, gasping and tasting.

Not wanting to pull out of the kiss, Tucker guided Ivan sideways toward the sofa. Together they stumbled, Tucker landing first on the plush cushions, Ivan on top of him and still in Tucker's grasp. The weight of Ivan's body pressed against Tucker's, and as they devoured each other, the bulge in Ivan's jeans rubbed against Tucker's groin.

Tucker reached up and framed Ivan's face in his hands, holding onto his head, carding his fingers through Ivan's short hair. He smelled of soap and cologne, and his tongue was minty, darting in and out of Tucker's mouth. God, how he wanted him. He wanted all of this young man, every fucking inch.

In one smooth movement, Tucker swung Ivan around and repositioned himself so that he was on top. With Ivan beneath him, Tucker kissed his way down Ivan's chin, onto his neck. Ivan squirmed and moaned as Tucker's lips found Ivan's erogenous zone.

Tucker grasped the tail of Ivan's polo shirt, pulling upward to expose his smooth, tight abdominals. Ivan pushed forward, raising his arms to allow Tucker to peel the shirt up his torso and over his head. He discarded it carelessly onto the floor and continued his descent down Ivan's body. He pressed his lips against one of Ivan's sensitive, brown nipples while kneading his other pectoral with his fingers.

"Oh damn!" Ivan bucked beneath him.

Tucker slid both hands down Ivan's body, trailing his way across the lean man's abs until he reached the buckle on Ivan's jeans. Hurriedly he unfastened the pants and peeled back Ivan's fly. Tucker backed up, allowing himself to slide off the couch onto his knees. He grasped the waistband of Ivan's underwear and tugged, peeling them down along with Ivan's jeans to reveal a steel-hard erection. Damn, his circumcised cock was as beautiful as the rest of him.

Without further hesitation, Tucker leaned in, opening his mouth, and took Ivan into his mouth. Ivan's hands gripped Tucker's shoulders as he swallowed the cock in one, smooth, downward stroke.

"Oh fuck!"

The velvety texture of the skin against Tucker's tongue made him all the more turned on. A spark of excitement ignited within him, blazing hotter than ever before, and he began to suck with ferocity. Bobbing up and down, he inhaled Ivan's throbbing cock. On the upstrokes he did his best to gulp air, but mostly he concentrated on pleasing his partner.

Tucker himself throbbed in his chinos as he took Ivan's cock to the root.

Ivan gasped and pushed hard on Tucker's shoulders. Tucker eased up, releasing some of the suction as he slid to the tip of Ivan's bulbous head. He stared up at him, using his eyes to convey what he couldn't say with his full mouth. Slowly he backed off, and as he did so, he peeled Ivan's jeans the rest of the way down his thighs and finally pulled them off to discard them alongside his forgotten shirt.

"Holy fuck." Ivan's eyes were wide as he stared down at Tucker. "Tucker…you're gonna make me…"

"Shh." Tucker placed his hands on the inner sides of Ivan's thighs and pressed them outward, splaying them wide. He lowered himself, pressing his lips against the heavy nutsac that rested beneath Ivan's massive hardon. Slowly he began to lick, lapping each of his balls with his tongue.

"Oh, oh, oh!" Ivan squirmed on the sofa, a bit ticklish perhaps, but his reaction only encouraged Tucker to continue. His tongue laved the pair of scrumptious *huevos* as he wrapped his fist around Ivan's pulsing cock.

After a few moments, Tucker worked his way back up the shaft, then stopped as his lips at last pressed against the spongy, mushroom-like head. He looked up once more into Ivan's eyes before opening his mouth and again swallowing him whole.

This time he went for broke, rhythmically sliding up and down while maintaining a perfect amount suction. He concentrated on the sensitive area just below the glans, that sweet spot near the tip of Ivan's cock. Ivan's response told him he'd identified Ivan's trigger. He continued to suck and bob while cupping Ivan's balls with one hand.

"Oh damn! Tucker… *God!* Tucker, I'm gonna…I'm gonna…!"

Tucker felt Ivan's cum pulse in his mouth as the load pumped into his shaft. Ivan's last word wasn't quite intelligible as his body trembled and he released a powerful jet of hot cum into Tucker's mouth. He sucked even more fiercely and slid all the way down Ivan's shaft, allowing him to drain himself into Tucker's throat.

As Tucker at last pulled back and released Ivan's cock from his mouth, Ivan's entire body trembled. "Holy shit…I've never…oh my God…I've never experienced anything…." He could barely breathe.

Tucker climbed Ivan's body, pressing himself against Ivan's nakedness and silenced Ivan's barely intelligible utterings with a passionate kiss.

"Mm." Ivan stared into his eyes as he held Tucker's head in both hands. "Now, my turn."

Tucker pulled back and shook his head. He reached down to his hardon, kneading it with his palm as a jolt of excitement made him shudder. He moaned as he stared into Ivan's eyes and erupted in his chinos.

Chapter Ten

They sat side-by-side, Tucker in his desk chair and Ivan using one of Tucker's kitchen chairs. Ivan slid his hand into Tucker's as Tucker used his other to control the mouse.

"The DVR software I have on this computer is identical to what we use at the police station," Tucker explained. "Each closed-circuit surveillance system has a specific number of cameras that are all synced together. When a time is range locked, it can be backed up onto a DVD, and it gives us access to all the cameras during that period."

"And this has what time period?" Ivan looked into his eyes.

"From one in the morning until five—a four hour time period, which is pretty much the maximum they can lock. It should be enough, though. Like I said, we just have to watch the one camera, the one out by the entrance."

He released Ivan's hand long enough to type in his password, then opened the program. Tucker then opened the appropriate file and a tic-tac-toe pattern of videos appeared on the screen. Each was labeled with the camera number and time stamp.

"Here's the one we need." Tucker moved the mouse to the motel entrance, clicking on the frame to enlarge it to full screen.

"Oh wow. I can't believe how much clearer that is."

Tucker nodded. "Are you sure you want to do this with me?"

"I'm positive." Ivan slid his hand onto Tucker's thigh. "I'm sorry I've been such an ass to you."

The corners of Tucker's mouth rose, but he looked straight ahead at the monitor. "You can't help yourself. You hate authority."

"Authority? Is that what you are?"

"Well, I *do* represent the law."

Ivan laughed and slipped his hand farther into Tucker's lap. He had changed into sweats after his little accident a few minutes prior. Ivan enjoyed the softness of the fabric and allowed his fingers to dance back and forth. "And I'm such a bad, bad boy."

"You're naughty, that's what you are."

Ivan pressed his palm against Tucker's package, massaging gently. Tucker grabbed his wrist and pulled it back. "Are you sure you want to be doing *that* now?" He looked Ivan in the eye.

Ivan grew serious. Of course, he didn't want to do that now. What was he thinking? He was watching video of the night his mother was murdered, and he was possibly about to see his father heading out to the scene of the crime. This was no time for hanky panky.

"You're right. Let's just watch it."

"Okay, I'll start this at a fairly decent speed, but slow enough to where we can stop it when we see a car approaching the exit."

"All right."

Tucker pressed the fast forward a couple times, and Ivan watched the seconds advance rapidly on the time stamp. The time continued to roll, starting at 1:00am and continuing onward. They watched the screen intently until a couple minutes later, when the time had gotten to 1:18, they detected movement. Tucker quickly clicked on the mouse, slowing the video to real time.

"That's not him," Ivan said. "It's a white car, and Dad drives a black Escalade."

Tucker waited patiently until the car got closer to the camera and froze the video. "Looks like a Chevy Cruze. I can't see the driver's face." He enlarged the video, zooming in on the front of the car. "This isn't a good angle."

"It's not Dad," Ivan repeated. "Whoever it is, is wearing a baseball cap. Dad doesn't even own one. And he wouldn't be caught dead driving a Chevy."

Tucker nodded. "Okay, let's just keep watching."

They sat for the next half hour watching the entrance. Not a single vehicle pulled into the lot, and no others left the premises.

"I don't get it," Tucker said, scrubbing a hand across his face.

"What do you mean, you don't get it? What's there to get?"

"It's just…well, I was pretty sure…"

"That my dad was guilty."

Tucker leaned back in his chair then looked over to Ivan. "I guess I kind of *was* pretty sure."

"And now?"

"And now I'm not. It seems like he does have a very airtight alibi. I mean, we know for certain he checked in that night, and we know he ordered a wake-up call from his room at one o'clock. He never left the motel after that point, so how could be over here in Fulton at the crime scene?"

"So he didn't do it!" Ivan could hardly contain himself. He wanted to leap up from the chair.

"But what about…?"

"All the circumstantial evidence?" Ivan smiled at him slyly. "Maybe that's all it is—circumstantial."

"I guess this means I'm back to square one in my investigation."

Ivan pushed his chair back and grabbed hold of one arm of Tucker's desk chair. With determination, he tugged, spinning the chair in his direction. Tucker, caught off guard, gazed at him quizzically. "What are you doing?"

Ivan slid onto the floor, kneeling between Tucker's legs. "I'm about to see once and for all if I can handle such a big piece of meat in my mouth."

~ ~ ~ ~ ~

Had Tucker just made love to Ivan...*twice*? Well, yeah, if blowjobs counted as lovemaking. It sure felt like it. He'd never been with anyone who'd made him feel the way Ivan just had in the den. Holy fuck, how was he ever going to be able to sit in that desk chair again without thinking about that experience? He'd forever be plagued with PTSD — post terrific sex dreams.

He stepped up behind Ivan at the kitchen counter and wrapped his arms around him, placing his palms against Ivan's flat, ribbed abs. Nuzzling his chin against Ivan's neck, he whispered into his ear. "You don't have to cook for me."

Ivan trembled just a bit, perhaps shivering in response to Tucker's razor stubble. He tilted his head slightly, continuing with his food prep as if Tucker wasn't even there. "I'm not cooking for you. I'm cooking for *us*."

"I can order out."

"Thanks to you, I've got to put in at least an extra hour or two at the gym this week. I don't trust you to order out."

Tucker kissed the side of Ivan's face as he pressed his entire body into Ivan's backside, spooning him. "What gym do you go to? Maybe we could go together."

"I don't actually have a gym membership." He leaned toward the sink and turned on the water. "We have a community gym in our apartment complex. It has all the equipment I need."

"Maybe I could join you—"

Ivan stepped away, then turned to face Tucker. "No offense, but can we, um…can we maybe just try to take things slow right now?" He pointed the knife he was holding toward Tucker as he spoke. "I mean, I'm not even sure what just happened. We were arguing, and then the next thing I knew…"

"Not the second time—when you went down on me."

"Well, yeah." He shrugged. "I, uh, kinda couldn't help myself. I was excited. And relieved."

"It's okay, Ivan." He slipped his hands into his pockets, feeling awkward all of a sudden. "I'm not sure what happened either, but I hope it wasn't a onetime thing."

"That's just it. Everything's so complicated, and I think maybe we weren't exactly thinking clearly. I let my dick do the thinking when I shouldn't have." He turned back to the counter and resumed chopping vegetables.

Tucker closed his eyes for a second, sighing. He leaned against the counter alongside Ivan. "You know, you're driving me crazy. I really do wish we could chalk this up to casual sex. Fuck, who wouldn't want a guy like you as a fuck buddy, but…"

"But I can't get you out of my head." Ivan looked at him again. "And that's what's fucked up most of all. Even if we weren't in this situation—you being a cop investigating the murder of my mother—there are like a million reasons why you and me don't go together. We don't fit, Tucker."

"Yeah, you're probably right."

"And what you said earlier about authority, it's true. I was raised to follow rules, respect the hierarchy, be obedient. And I hate it. Most of the people I know in law enforcement are arrogant and hypocritical, and I can't see myself ever getting into any kind of serious relationship with a cop."

"I feel the same way about people who constantly judge me and who are always preaching at me."

"Preaching at you?" He set down the knife and turned off the faucet. "I haven't even *begun* to preach at you." He walked over to the stove and removed a kitchen towel, using it to wipe his hands. "You know why cops tend to be so conservative? Because they represent the status quo. They exist to make sure everyone follows the rules, to ensure that everything stays in line, nothing changes."

"How can you assume all police officers are conservative?"

"Do you believe in absolute values? Do you look at the law as a matter of right and wrong?"

"The law is the law…"

"And you follow the law no matter what."

"I'm a fucking officer *of* the law. Of course, I follow it no matter what."

"Which is why we don't fit, and why we'll *never* fit. I don't see things that way. I want to do whatever I can to help people, to understand and empathize with them. I don't see human beings as being all good or all evil, but I think there is goodness in almost everyone."

"What about your mother's killer?" As the words slipped out of his mouth, Tucker already regretted saying them.

Ivan stared at him, incredulous, then threw the towel onto the counter. "Maybe you should just drive me back to my car. I'm not really hungry anymore."

Tucker took a step closer. "Ivan, wait. I'm sorry."

"We don't even fucking know *who* my mother's killer is!" He pointed his finger angrily. "But as soon as *you* do your job and catch the guy, then I'll answer your fucking question! You know what? That's so not fair. That's so fucking low, for you to bring that up…"

"I'm sorry, Ivan…wait, please. You're right. I shouldn't have used that as an example. I'm just saying, sometimes it is a clear-cut matter of right and wrong. Whoever killed your mom should be in jail. And yes, it's my job to catch the killer, and I'm not going to stop until I have."

Ivan's eyes brimmed with tears, but he just stared straight ahead, not even blinking. "Please, just take me back to my car. I really need to go home."

Chapter Eleven

"I'm such a hypocrite." Ivan sat at Carrie's kitchen counter on one of her barstool chairs, shoveling a loaded tortilla chip from his Nacho Belle Grande into his mouth. "I bitched at him...*made fun of* him even...for eating crap, and look at me."

Carrie shrugged as she reached across the counter and stole a chip from his tray. "Everyone gets the munchies after smoking."

In a state of confused anger after he picked up his car from the diner parking lot, he'd headed over to Carrie's, arriving a couple hours earlier than their planned movie night. He'd spilled his guts, rambling incoherently about everything that had happened. He told her how Tucker had kissed him the night before, and how they'd gone on the road trip that morning and had finally given each other blowjobs back at Tucker's house.

As he explained everything, especially the part about how Tucker had gotten the video that all but cleared Ivan's father of murder, Ivan sounded like a lunatic to himself. He'd gotten all freaked out over petty bullshit, and once again, he'd made assumptions about Tucker that weren't necessarily true.

Carrie knew exactly how to handle the situation. She dragged Ivan out onto the patio and fired up a jay, which they shared before heading to Taco Bell. Her husband and daughter, Madison, wouldn't be home for another hour or so, at which time family movie night would commence.

"Of course you're not going to see everything the same way." She licked a dollop of sour cream from her finger. "What couple does?"

"We're not a couple. We'll *never* be a couple." Ivan carefully selected the largest, unbroken chip, which was slathered with melty nacho cheese, and shoved the entire thing into his mouth.

"Nobody's saying you have to marry him, Ivy. But you can't deny the man's gorgeous. Holy shit, he's fucking sex on legs. Can't you at least appreciate the physical beauty? You know, you don't have to talk politics and philosophy while fucking."

"You're saying I should just be his fuck buddy."

Again, she shrugged. "What's wrong with that? As long as you're safe and not cheating on anyone…"

"You know what it is? It's not that there's anything specific about him that is over-the-top horrible. It's not like he has some grotesque flaw that I that can't overlook. It's *me*. I can't stop hating myself for being attracted to a guy like him."

She laughed. "Please don't expect me to do psycho analysis when I'm high."

"Carrie, in many ways Tucker represents the kind of man who's always given me shit. All the hyper masculine, gun toting men in my parent's church — my Dad — *Liam*. They're all the same. I don't want to be involved with someone like that again. Why do I find myself attracted to men with way too much testosterone?"

"Because they're men! You dummy. Now you know what women feel like. It's nature. We're attracted to the very things we hate about them. I can't stand Bryan's arrogance. I tell him all the time he's being an ass, but at the same time I find his confidence sexy."

Ivan rolled his eyes. "It's not the same thing. Bryan's about the nicest straight guy on the planet. He's the opposite of Tucker."

"He puts on a good show when you're in the room. Trust me, he's every bit the chauvinist pig as every other man on the planet. He's a man, and men are imperfect creatures. It's only because I love him so much that I choose to forgive him for the thousand little ways he's hurt me."

"Aw." Ivan took hold of her hand. "Bryan's hurt you?"

"Of course he's hurt me, but hardly ever on purpose. He's talked down to me, mansplained, corrected, dismissed me. You name it. And he doesn't even realize when he's doing it unless I stop him and point it out. You know why? Because it's a man's world. For centuries women have been treated like they're property, the helpmates of men, created from a man's rib."

Ivan shook his head, smiling. "Oh brother. You're right, we shouldn't talk philosophy when we're high."

"I said don't ask me to psycho analyze you when I'm high. Being stoned is the *perfect* time to talk philosophy."

"Okay fine. I hear what you're saying, but guess what? I'm a man too."

"Oh honey." She smiled as if to humor him.

"Carrie! I'm being serious. What if I do all these things myself? You said Bryan does it without even realizing it. What if I talk down to people, exercise my white male privilege?"

"Well, yeah, you do, but probably less than the average straight guy. And who knows, maybe less than a guy like Tucker. He *is* a police officer, and it's kind of a prerequisite of the job that he have an ego and know how to use it."

"This whole thing is crazy. Why's it even matter? It's not like we can have any sort of long lasting relationship. In fact, we can't even be open about what we have now…which is practically nothing. But if word gets out that we've been involved in any way, he could be in big trouble at his job. There's kind of a conflict of interest here, ya know."

"The case won't go on forever, and now that he knows your father was not involved in the crime, he will probably just hand it off to someone else."

"No! He'd better not."

Carrie laughed. "Ivy, he can hardly continue investigating a crime involving your family when you and him are…"

"We're not! It was a one-time thing, and a mistake. I don't want someone else taking over the case."

"Okay, now you're delusional." She stepped around the counter and placed her hand on his shoulder. "About this being a one-time thing, I mean. You don't spend two hours spilling your guts about a guy to your best friend over a joint and a coma-inducing lethal plate of nachos if you're not ever going to be fucking him again."

Ivan scowled. "We didn't fuck yet." His voice was almost a whisper. "Unfortunately."

~ ~ ~ ~ ~

Jesus Christ, if there was one thing Tucker knew how to do better than anything else it was to ruin a good thing. He'd really stepped in it this time. Everything had been going fine, and then all of a sudden, he said the wrong thing. He never meant to hurt Ivan, though. Cripes, he didn't even mean to offend him. He was just trying to show that in some cases people were bad. People did awful things, and they deserved to face the consequences of their actions. He saw it every day. It was his job to catch these criminals and lock them up.

But Ivan had a point about cops being power-hungry pricks. Tucker had known more than a few arrogant police officers who had let their authority go to their heads. And yes, they did represent the status quo. Their job was to enforce the law, as written. Changing the law to make things fairer—that was an entirely different thing. A lot of people didn't understand this. They blamed cops for shitty laws, but it wasn't any more his fault that a law was poorly written than it was the cashier's fault at Walmart for their bullshit return policy.

He did have some leeway, though. He could selectively enforce the laws, turn a blind eye to minor offenses that he didn't deem worth his time. He could give people warnings instead of being hardnosed and overly strict about every little letter of the law. He could make a conscious choice to view situations more broadly and holistically, remaining more within the spirit of the law than dogmatically following rigid guidelines.

Perhaps that's the point Ivan was trying to make, and Tucker got it. He could discuss these topics reasonably. He could understand nuance, but for some reason, he and Ivan always managed to clash. Why did they have to lock horns on everything? Tucker didn't expect Ivan to agree with him on everything, so why did Ivan expect Tucker to do so?

He really didn't know what the fuck he was doing in the kitchen, but Ivan had started this stir fry. He'd nearly completed all the prep and had every ingredient lying out on the counter, so why not just finish it? He should call Janelle and ask her how much peanut oil to use. He picked up the bottle and read the side, hoping for instructions. No, if he called Janelle, she'd grill him about what had happened, and she'd assume he was being an ass again.

She'd also scold him for not calling Brianna. He really needed to recuse himself from the case, and after what had happened this afternoon between Ivan and him—their intimacy—he couldn't exactly continue to be objective. Well, that's how they'd see it anyway. Brianna certainly would.

I guess I should cook up the chicken breast first. Do I deep fry it in this oil?

Oh fuck, he didn't know what the hell he was doing. He stormed out of the kitchen and back into the den where he pulled up YouTube. He typed in the words "chicken stir fry" and several videos populated. *If only there were videos on how to win over the heart of a headstrong, know-it-all pediatric nurse who was cute as fuck and who could suck golf balls through a garden hose…*

He watched a few minutes of the cooking video. The online chef made it look so easy. He picked up the laptop and carried it back to the kitchen. He set it on the countertop next to his ingredients and restarted the video, then proceeded, step-by-step to follow the instructions.

When he finished, his stir fry wasn't nearly as presentable as the dish in the video, but it was good, and he was proud of himself. He then went on to clean up his kitchen and even managed to sweep and mop the floor. Ivan would proud of him…maybe.

He nodded resolutely. "I can cook if I put my mind to it. And clean. And I can even do a better job parenting. Ivan's right. I need to start feeding Jaydin more than just chicken tenders and peanut butter and jelly sandwiches."

He'd show Ivan that he wasn't the redneck buffoon Ivan had assumed him to be. He might be shallow and at times stubborn, but he hadn't just fallen off the turnip truck yesterday. And he'd figure out how to win over Ivan's trust all the while solving the mystery of this murder. He could do it. He knew he could.

He stepped back over to his laptop and typed in a search term in his browser. And he'd start winning that trust right now. *Floral deliveries.*

~ ~ ~ ~ ~

Ivan stopped momentarily at the nurse's station to take in the huge spray of roses. Usually his patients received smiley-faced and heart-shaped balloon bouquets or stuffed animals. Big arrangements of flowers were a rarity in the pediatric ward. He leaned in to smell them, and then as he pulled back and opened his mouth to speak, he caught a glimpse of his name on the card extending from the bouquet.

"What?" He gasped and held one hand over his chest. "Carrie! Carrie! What is this?"

She stepped out from the office and walked up to the counter. "Looks like someone has an admirer."

"No way. This can't be real!"

"It's real, you doofus. Read the card." She pointed insistently.

Suddenly he grew serious. "Oh wait. I bet it's someone sending their condolence about my mom. They were probably late hearing about it."

"Well, I doubt it. Red roses? Not usually what one sends for a funeral. But you'll never find out if you don't open the damn card."

Rolling his eyes, he snatched the card from its holder and opened the envelope. He removed the business-sized card to read the inscription. "Forgive me for last night. You're amazing...and right about everything. Love, T — P.S. I finished the stir fry. Turned out delicious."

"Oh my God. Carrie, what am I gonna do?" He thrust the card into her hand.

"I think you're going to be smelling roses for the next few days." She read the card. "Aw, this is sweet. Ivan, I think he really adores you. And look, he signed it 'Love'."

"That doesn't mean anything."

A couple other workers stopped, staring at the flowers. "Wow, who got the flowers?"

"Ivan!" Carrie didn't seem to know the meaning of discretion. "From his looover!" She said the word slowly, exaggerating the vowel sound.

"He's not my lover."

"Ivan, you've got a boyfriend!" One of the nurses, middle aged and portly with glasses, clapped her hands gleefully. Darleen was the type always bragging about her grandbabies. It seemed funny to see her so excited about a gay romance.

Wait, this wasn't a romance. They'd only spent a single afternoon together. They'd engaged in a little hanky panky — no big deal. "You're making too much of this."

"Ivan, tell us about him!" Darleen rubbed her hands together. "And don't spare the juicy details."

He raised both hands in the air, shaking his head in protest. "There *are* no juicy details to tell. We just spent one afternoon together. He bought me a root beer float."

"That right there." Carrie removed a pen from her ear and used it to point at Ivan. "That should tell you all you need to know. If a man bought me a root beer float, he'd *own* my heart."

"Shut up, all of you!" Ivan grinned. "There's nothing to see here. Go away. Go do some work or something. Give a shot. Change a bedpan. Just get the fuck away from me!"

Once the crowd dispersed, Ivan leaned in and smelled the roses, closing his eyes as he did so. Now what? What did he do at this point?

Chapter Twelve

"I thought I had it figured out." Tucker sat with his partner in the evidence room, reviewing the DVR one more time. "Motive, weapon, timeline...they all line up. But this alibi blows everything out of the fucking water."

Vivano shrugged. "He hired someone to do it."

"But how? I've gone through all his financial records."

"He hasn't paid them yet, maybe?" The detective leaned in, staring at the screen, and rubbed his chin. "Maybe we're not going to solve this until we can follow the money. He probably hired someone to off his wife, but he's not paying until he gets the insurance money."

"Or he paid them some other way. I mean, I hardly think he'd write a fucking check."

Viviano chuckled. "Go through his cancelled checks and look for 'assassination fee' in the memo lines."

Tucker pushed himself up and paced a couple times across the width of the small room. He scrubbed one hand over his face. "It's not that what you're saying isn't plausible. It makes perfect sense, but my gut is telling me something else. I know he did it. I can *feel* it."

Viviano smiled and raised both hands in the air. "And to hell with the presumption of innocence, due process, and all that nonsense. Let's just go arrest him, and you can explain to the judge you had a feeling."

"Shut up." Tucker scowled, but Viviano was right. He had to go where the evidence took him. He couldn't go around targeting suspects on the basis of intuition for lack of hardcore evidence.

"You know I'm right. We need evidence, man."

Tucker sighed and plopped back down in the chair. "Let's watch it again. Reset the video at where the white car leaves."

"We've already watched this a dozen times."

"Just do it! Humor me."

~ ~ ~ ~ ~

Ivan's twelve-hour night shift ended Tuesday morning, and he wanted nothing more than to just head home and hit the hay for a few hours. He'd have to be back to work that night since it was only the first of his three day stretch. Carrying his huge arrangement of roses, he walked briskly across the parking structure toward his car but suddenly stopped in his tracks.

"Brandon…" His brother stood beside Ivan's car, obviously waiting for him.

"We need to talk. Wanna have breakfast with me?"

"Um, sure. Let me put these in the backseat. You want to meet me somewhere or ride with me?"

"I'm parked across the street at that Coney restaurant. We can just walk over if you want to eat there."

Ivan shrugged. "Why not."

"Where'd you get the flowers?"

Ivan placed the roses in the backseat and closed the door, then depressed his key fob to lock the car. He turned to his brother. "Oh, a friend sent them."

"Someone you're dating?"

He shook his head. "No, not really. Just a friend."

"Someone I know?"

"I don't think so." Ivan didn't wait for another response but started walking back toward the parking structure exit. "Actually, I was going to call you. I met with that detective, the one investigating the fire. He showed me a video I wanted to tell you about."

"That's kind of what I wanted to talk you about."

Ivan stopped in his tracks and turned to his brother. "What? You met with Tucker?"

"Tucker?"

"The detective. Tucker Brown."

"Oh, no. I didn't meet with anyone. You two are on a first-name basis now?"

Ivan turned away and resumed walking. "No, I just remembered that's what his name was. What do you mean, you wanted to talk to me about the video."

"Not the video—the investigation. We need to figure out what we're going to do before Dad gets back from Florida. He's going to be home on Saturday."

They'd reached the sidewalk outside the parking structure. Ivan stepped up to the crosswalk and pressed the button.

"Come on, there's nothing coming." Brandon stepped out into the street. Ivan almost called after him to stop. There was a reason for crosswalks, and he normally didn't jaywalk. Cripes, he was sometimes worse than Tucker. He stepped briskly, hurrying to catch up to his brother.

When they got inside the restaurant, they chose a booth and both ordered breakfast. "Well, let me tell you about the video," Ivan said. "Detective Brown went to the motel where dad was staying the night of the fire. He'd placed a call from his room to the front desk around one o'clock. So we watched the video from one until the early hours of the morning. Dad never left the room. There's no way he could have done it, Brandon. He was at the motel, and his alibi is air tight."

Brandon leaned forward, staring intently at his younger brother. "I can't believe the police would have shown that to you."

"They're trying to find out who murdered mom. Why's it matter if they showed it to me? It just proves Dad didn't do it."

"Then what's he doing in Florida with Diana Seavers?"

Ivan shrugged. "Let's face it, he probably was cheating on Mom, and that's horrible. It's something we're going to have to work through, but that doesn't make him a murderer."

"And the life insurance...and the diamond ring. What about them?"

"I think we should just flat-out confront him on everything. If he bought the ring for Mom, I think we should ask him for it. We can do something with it."

Brandon looked at him like he was from outer space. "What do you mean?"

"I mean, like we can sell it and use the money for something to honor Mom's memory."

"He'd never agree to that."

"He *should*. If he bought the ring for her, he should want it to memorialize her."

Brandon took a sip of his coffee. "I highly doubt he bought it for her, and it's probably already on that other woman's finger. Ivan, I don't think I can have him staying with me. He's going to have to figure something else out, rent a motel room or something."

"Or move in with his girlfriend." Ivan scowled. "Look, I don't blame you. I don't want him to live with me either, and I can probably never forgive him for what he did...what he's *doing*. But he's still our dad, and..."

The waitress arrived with their breakfast. Ivan had simply chosen a bowl of oatmeal and wheat toast. He picked up one of the slices and took a bite.

"You call that breakfast?" Brandon tossed an entire strip of bacon into his mouth.

"I don't think Dad would be capable of killing another human being, especially not Mom." It felt bizarre to be talking about this so casually. "Now that I think about it, I'm not surprised he didn't do it. The affair is what confused me."

"I don't know, Ivy."

"Please don't call me that." Ivan glared at his big brother. "I'm not five anymore."

"Alright, *Ivan*." Brandon smiled, and his expression felt so sincere. "This whole thing sucks. I feel like we've lost both our parents, ya know. I mean, even if Dad is not guilty, he isn't the man I thought he was."

Ivan nodded. "But people have affairs. Marriages end every day and people fall out of love. If Mom hadn't died, we'd probably still eventually have to deal with Dad having this girlfriend, possibly divorcing Mom."

"How convenient that he doesn't have to worry about that. He not only gets to avoid a messy divorce but he gets a shit ton of insurance."

"Brandon, that's not fair, is it? He still was with Mom all those years. They still loved each other, and I believe his grief was real."

"I hope you're right." Brandon swallowed hard, and for a second it seemed like he might be about to tear up. "I think a lot of that whole process — the funeral and everything — was for show, for the church people."

"No." Ivan shook his head defiantly. "I disagree. Dude, Mom really believed in all that. And when I had lunch with her the day before she died, I believe she was really worried about me. It's not so much that she hated that I'm gay, it's that she feared for me. She didn't want me to lose my salvation or whatever. If anyone on earth really and truly believed, it was her."

"She did worry about you." Brandon looked him right in the eye. "But she also worried too much about other people and what they would think of her having a gay son."

A wave of emotion swept over Ivan, and his eyes instantly moistened. "Please don't. I'm not ready to hear bad things about her."

"I'm not speaking ill of the dead. I'm just stating facts."

"Well, I'm not ready for that! I might never be."

Brandon reached across the table, placing his hand on his brother's arm. "Like I told you to begin with, I honestly think she would have come around. She'd have worked through her feelings and eventually accepted you for who you truly are. I'm just sayin, that religion kind of messed her up."

Ivan picked up his napkin and wiped his eyes. "Why do you do this? I haven't cried once in the past forty-eight hours. I thought I was making progress. And look at me—you've reduced me to tears."

"I'm sorry."

Ivan looked at him, smiling through his tears. "It's okay. You're the one person in our family who's always loved me. You've always had my back, and you've always protected me."

"Tell me who sent you the flowers." Brandon grinned mischievously. "It must be kind of serious."

"No." Ivan waved a hand dismissively and laughed. "It's really not. I mean, I don't think so, but given a different set of circumstances, maybe it could be."

"What do you mean?"

"There's just too much going on right now. This is a really bad time for me to try to deal with a relationship...or dating...or anything like that."

"Maybe this is the best time. Ivan, you need someone right now."

"Plus, he infuriates me."

Brandon leaned back and laughed. "He must be as headstrong as you, then."

"Way more. Oh my God, you have no idea. Honestly, he's not my type. He's too...I don't know...*masculine*."

"Too masculine? I thought you liked butch guys."

"I do! Maybe that's not the word. He's too *macho*. Too much testosterone. He's like the sort of guy you'd never in a million years suspect of being gay."

"Straight acting."

Ivan squinted, giving him the evil eye. "That's one of those terms you really shouldn't be using."

"I've heard you use it a million times."

"And I can. Just like I can call my gay friends 'fags'. There are certain things that are all right for gay people to say that straight people shouldn't. When you say a gay guy is 'straight acting' you sound like you mean he's 'normal'. And that's offensive."

"Whatever." He rolled his eyes. "I don't even know what that means, to be honest. What's normal? And why are certain behaviors considered gay and others straight?"

"Exactly! That's my point. When gay guys talk amongst ourselves, we say a guy is 'straight' acting because he defies all the heteronormative stereotypes. He doesn't like show tunes or opera, he follows sports and knows nothing about fashion or interior decorating."

"And that' show this new love interest of yours is?"

"He's *not* a love interest!" Ivan couldn't help himself, he beamed from ear to ear. "Well, not officially."

Brandon pointed his finger and winked. "I want to meet him."

"No way."

"Yes, you said yourself I've always been your protector."

"I don't need this kind of protection. I can make my own decisions when it comes to my love — or I mean, my *social* life."

Brandon laughed. "Already using the L word."

"Can we go back to grieving or something? Anything but this topic…"

"I'm giving you a week. If you don't reveal this mystery man to me in the next seven days, I'm going to find him on my own."

"Brandon, please."

"I mean it."

Ivan sighed. He loved how supportive and protective his brother was, but Brandon was going to shit his pants when he found out Ivan's "romantic interest" was the police detective, Tucker Brown.

Chapter Thirteen

Kneeling in one of the chairs at the dining room table, Jaydin picked up the box of sixty-four crayons and dumped them into an enormous pile. Tucker looked up from his laptop at the chaos, and opened his mouth to speak, then stopped.

"I need the other blue," Jaydin said, scowling as he stared down at the pile. "This is wrong. I want blue like the sky!"

Tucker pushed his laptop aside and began sorting through the crayons. "Probably didn't have to dump them all out like this."

"I had to, Daddy. I couldn't see them."

He glanced over at his son's construction paper. "I see. If you use the darker blue, it will look like nighttime."

"But it's not nighttime. Look, the sun is shining." He pointed to the sun in the upper right corner of the picture, shining through the window.

"What about this one?" Tucker picked up one of the crayons and examined it, reading the inscription on the side. "Sky blue. Sounds perfect."

Jaydin beamed and snatched the crayon from his father. "Thanks, Daddy!"

"Who's that a picture of?"

Jaydin tilted his head slightly, staring at the nearly completed project. "Can't you tell? It's me when I had my operation."

"Oh right. Yeah, I see it now. And that's Mommy…and me. Who's that?" He pointed to the other figure in the drawing. "That's not Dr. Warren. She's a woman." The character, presumably male, wore a stethoscope around his neck.

"My friend Ivan. Don't you remember? He's my other doctor."

Tucker smiled and nodded. "Oh yeah, I remember, but Ivan's not a doctor. He was your nurse."

"Cause boys can be nurses too. And girls can be doctors. Before—a long time ago before I was born—not very many doctors were girls."

"That's right, but things have changed."

"And I can be anything I want, even if it's a nurse."

"Exactly, just like Ivan."

"Or a policeman like you, Daddy."

Tucker reached over and closed his laptop as Jaydin finished coloring in the sky on his picture. Tucker had spent enough time pouring over his cases all day. After dropping Jaydin off at pre-school, he'd put in a full nine hours without a lunch break before he had to at last go pick his son up from daycare. That only left them a few hours together in the evening, so why was he wasting his precious time staring at his laptop?

He grabbed a coloring book from the stack at the side of the table.

"Yay! You're going to color with me?" Jaydin pushed his finished artwork aside and selected a coloring book of his own.

"You're probably a better colorer than me." Tucker laughed. "I haven't used crayons in years."

"I can teach you!"

As strange as it sounded, Jaydin was probably right. Tucker had never really possessed any sort of artistic talent. A four-year-old probably *could* teach him a thing or two about coloring.

"You have to stay between the lines," Jaydin explained. "But it's for fun, so it don't matter if you make a mistake. If you mess up, just color over it with a dark color."

Tucker laughed. "You learn that from Mommy?"

"Yup." He grinned. "And it doesn't matter what colors you use. You pick whatever kind you want, whatever you think looks good."

"What if I want to color this dog pink?" He pointed to his page.

Jaydin giggled. "A pink dog? That's funny, Daddy. Or purple, if you want. It's only for fun, you know, like make believe. In the make believe world there can be pink and purple dogs."

Before Tucker could respond, the door bell interrupted them. Tucker looked up at the wall clock. It was almost seven o'clock, and he wasn't expecting anyone. "Wonder who that is…"

Unfazed, Jaydin continued to flip through his coloring book, looking for the perfect picture to choose. Tucker pushed his chair back and walked across the living room into the foyer, and then to the front door. He peered through the glass on the door to see who it was, and then paused. *Son of a bitch. Really?* He pulled open the door.

"Ivan! What're you doing here?"

Wearing his scrubs and smelling like a breath of fresh air, he smiled sweetly. "I got your flowers, and I had to stop and thank you."

"Well, come on in…please." He stepped aside to allow Ivan entry.

"I can't stay — on my way to work. My shift starts at nine."

"Ivan!" Jaydin ran across the living room into the foyer and rushed up to his favorite nurse, hugging him as Ivan squatted down to greet him. "Why are you here at my house?"

"I came to see you and your daddy."

Jaydin pulled back and stared up at his father, his eyes growing wide with concern. "Daddy, do I have to go back to the hospital?"

"No, baby." Tucker reached down and caressed the back of his son's head, laughing gently. "Ivan's just here for a visit. He's our friend."

"Ivan, do you want to color with us?" Jaydin bounced with excitement, clapping his hands. "And…and…and…" He looked at his father. "Daddy, can I give Ivan my picture?"

"Of course."

"And I made you a picture! Wanna see it?"

Ivan rose to his feet, now holding Jaydin's hand. "You bet I do."

"Come on!" Ivan allowed himself to be pulled across the kitchen into the dining room.

"Jaydin, slow down," his father cautioned. "And it's almost bedtime."

"But we have company!" Jaydin's lower lip protruded as he stopped at the table and looked up at the two grown-ups. He slid back onto his chair, leaning across the table, and retrieved his construction-paper artwork. He climbed down from the chair and thrust it into Ivan's hand. "Here! Do you like it?"

"I do! This is awesome." Ivan looked down at the picture. "This is you, in the hospital, right?"

"Yup! And Mommy and Daddy…and *you*!" He pointed to the smiling nurse.

"I'm glad I'm smiling."

"Cause you're always smiling, silly. Like right now."

Ivan and Tucker both laughed. "Is this for me to keep?"

"Yes! It's a present."

"Oh my gosh." Ivan's smile softened as he raised one hand to his chest. "Really? I love it. Thank you so much."

"Get a coloring book! Pick out any one you want and you can color a picture with Daddy and me."

"Daddy's going to color a picture too?" Ivan turned to Tucker, offering a look of mock seriousness.

"Honey, Ivan can't stay very long. He has to go to work tonight, and it's almost time for your bath…and bed."

"But you said we could color together."

"Why don't we have Ivan over later this week, maybe Friday?"

"I'll be at my other house on Friday…with Mommy."

"Not this week, remember? You stayed at Mommy's last weekend."

"Oh, right!"

"Know what I heard?" Ivan turned to Jaydin and leaned forward. "I heard there's going to be a carnival this weekend. Maybe we could go together. I have the weekend off again."

"Can we, Daddy?"

"Sounds like a lot of fun." He turned to Ivan. "If that's what you want to do."

"I definitely want to." Ivan glanced back and forth between them. "And I wish I could stay tonight to color with you, kiddo. But I have to go to work. I love my picture, though, and I'm going to hang up in my work station."

"For everyone to see!"

"That's right." He reached down to ruffle Jaydin's hair.

"Jay, why don't you start picking up these crayons and putting them back in the box? I'll walk Ivan out."

"We're not done coloring! You didn't even start your pink dog, Daddy."

Ivan grinned. "When you get it done, I want to see it. I'll definitely hang than one up at work."

"We can color again some other time. I didn't realize how late it was getting, and we have to get your bath before bed."

"There's too many crayons to pick up." Jaydin pouted as he stared at the mountain of colors on the table.

"Well, you did it, mister. You made the mess. Start picking them up, and when I come back inside, I'll help you finish."

Jaydin sighed dramatically. "Okay."

As Tucker and Ivan stepped outside the front door, Tucker walked him down the steps and then a few paces toward his car. "Thank you for stopping over."

Ivan turned to him. "I was kind of a jerk Sunday. You've gone out of your way—above and beyond what anyone could expect—to be helpful to me and my family. I know I get defensive sometimes."

Tucker placed a hand on Ivan's shoulder. "You're going through so much right now, and you didn't say anything that wasn't true. I do tend to see things in very black-and-white terms, and it helps me to hear other perspectives."

Ivan laughed. "Now you're just being nice."

With a shrug, Tucker nodded. "Maybe, but you're worth being nice to, and I don't want to screw things up by being…well, by being *me*."

"I want you to be you," Ivan whispered. "I like you the way you are, and a lot of what I was saying comes from in here." He pointed to his chest. "I have my own baggage, and I've been hurt before. I think I've been afraid you'd end up being like the others, that you'd hurt me the same way I've been hurt in the past."

"I hope I never hurt you."

"I know, but it wasn't fair of me. If you'll forgive me, I'd like to start over. I'd like to get to know the real you — apart from all the stereotypes."

"Ivan..." Tucker sighed. "Will you please just shut up?"

Ivan stared at him as Tucker leaned in and kissed him. Wrapping their arms around one another, they fused into a tender embrace. Their passion rapidly intensified as Tucker opened his mouth and kissed Ivan fervently.

When he pulled back, Ivan continued to gaze into his eyes. "Wow," he whispered.

"So I'll see you Friday?"

Ivan nodded but didn't move from where he was standing. Like a statue, he stood there holding the construction paper artwork in one hand and the other hand over his heart.

"See you then." Tucker turned and headed back up the walk. As he did so, he saw movement at the window. A little man had been standing on the other side of the door, his face barely poking up onto the glass, but when he saw his daddy coming back inside, he darted back into the dining room.

Oh geez, maybe I'm going to need to have that conversation with Jaydin sooner than I planned.

~ ~ ~ ~ ~

"Britany, Rhianna, Gaga, Katy, Christina..." Ivan stood sorting through his CD collection, trying to decide what to play, as Dustin rummaged through the walk-in closet.

"Gay!"

"Mariah, Whitney, Cher, Madonna, Cyndi..."

"Gayer!"

"Bette, Aretha, Barbra…"

"Gayest! Good Lord, do you have your CD's arranged from least to greatest divas, or what?"

"Shut up, Dusty. I have them arranged by decade."

"Oh my God, you are so fucking OCD. Look at this closet! Everything's color-coordinated. Look at these shirts." Ivan stepped over to the threshold of the closet as Dustin pointed to the left side of the rack. Using his hand like Vanna White, he waved it across the display of clothing. "White, off-white, cream, beige, tan, brown—"

"Ecru and taupe, *not* off-white and cream."

"What-the-fuck-ever! Who the hell does this? Honey, you *need* this date more than I can even say. You've got to have something more important in your life than color-coordinating your clothes and arranging your CDs by diva birth year."

"It's not a date. I'm going to a carnival…with a four year old." He pulled off one of the short-sleeved shirts from the rack. "How about this? With a sweater, in case it gets chilly."

"Forget the sweater." Dustin waved his hand dismissively. "If you catch a chill, your man can take off his jacket and wrap it around your shoulders."

Ivan couldn't resist an eyeroll. "First of all, he's not 'my man'." He raised his hand to make air quotes. "That's not what I'm looking for, some big macho dude to protect me and treat me like his teenage girlfriend."

Dustin raised one finger to his chin and nodded slightly as he stared intently at Ivan. "Did you lose your gay card again? Let me call the 800 number and order you a replacement."

"I've been thinking about this a lot." Ivan turned toward the back wall and pulled off a sweater from the rack, examining it against the shirt he was still holding. "Part of my problem in the past is that I've been looking for that kind of relationship. I've been trying to find the perfect man, my knight in shining armor — my hero. But you know what?" He spun around to face Dustin. "I don't need a hero. I don't need someone to save me, to be every bit the man I wish I could be myself. Dusty, I *am* a man. I'm a man dating another man, not a girl in a man's body."

Dustin just stared at him, dumbfounded. "Well then…"

"Wait! I didn't mean — "

Dustin had already turned and walked back into the bedroom. Ivan followed.

"Dusty, please wait. You know you're my best friend."

"Am I?" He turned to face Ivan again. "Even though I act like a girl in a man's body?"

"Yes! That's not an insult. I mean, come on. Look at us. I'm exactly the same in many ways. I'm just not as…uh…*fluid* as you."

"You think you're not as nelly and swishy."

Ivan sighed, relaxing his shoulders. "No, that's not what I was saying. I really don't care about that. I love how swishy and nelly you are, but…How do I even explain this? When I'm with Tucker, he doesn't make me feel like a delicate flower. He doesn't condescend, remind me that he's more masculine than me. I don't feel like I'm his trophy or his property."

"How can you even know that yet?"

"Well, that's a good question. We haven't really even gone out yet, but so far…"

"I get what you're saying, Ivy." Dustin took a step closer to him, extending one arm to snatch the hanger Ivan was holding. "This sweater is ghastly. You're right. You and I are not alike when it comes to our preference in men. I totally want to be dominated, to be every bit aware of the contrast between us. His masculinity makes me *feel* more feminine, and I love it."

Ivan nodded repeatedly. "Yes, I get that too. And yet, when it comes to you and me, I do feel like we're girlfriends, not boyfriends."

"Duh!"

"I relate to the campy, fem part of you. I have some of that within me. It's just mine is a bit more reserved. A bit more…" He took a step backward across the threshold. "…closeted."

Dustin laughed. "Alright then, let's pick out something that says 'confidence and manliness'." He steered Ivan farther into the closet, stepping in behind him. "And a pair of pants that show off that perfect, fuckable ass of yours."

Chapter Fourteen

Janelle had picked Jaydin up from daycare Wednesday evening according to schedule, so Tucker had two days alone at his house before the big date. He was supposed to stop and get Jaydin from Janelle's Friday after work, and then they were going to the carnival. Instead of heading to his ex's, though, Tucker went straight home after work. He had to get ready, and then he'd run over to get Jaydin before Ivan arrived.

Why was he making such a big deal of this? It wasn't like this was an official date or anything. He didn't even have to dress up. In fact, it would be absurd if he did dress up. He just needed to throw on a t-shirt and pair of jeans and be done with it.

Yet he spent a good forty-five minutes in the bathroom, showering, shaving, combing and re-combing his hair. When his phone's ringtone finally sounded, he jolted back to reality and snatched it off the bathroom counter.

"Hello, Janelle."

"Forget something?"

"I didn't forget. I'm on my way."

"Your son is waiting, and not very patiently. Would have been nice of you to call to let us know you're running late."

"I'm not..." He held out his phone to check the time. "Oh shit, I *am* late. Sorry. I'll be there in ten."

"With your boyfriend?"

"What?" Tucker blanched as he stared at his reflection in the mirror. "Who told you that?"

"A little bird...aka our son." She laughed. "Jay said Ivan's going to the carnival with you."

"Is that okay?" He hadn't even considered checking with Janelle first. After all, she was the one who'd suggested he pursue Ivan.

"Of course it's okay. Just like it's okay for me to introduce him to any guy I'm dating if I feel comfortable doing so."

Tucker scowled at his own reflection, then turned away from the mirror. He wasn't so sure he liked the sound of that. He wanted to know about any man in his son's life. Then again, Janelle had a point. It wasn't about whether or not he approved of whom Janelle exposed Jaydin to. It was about trust. He trusted her to put the wellbeing of their son first, and obviously she trusted him as well.

"Alright, I'm at my house. I had to change after work, but I'm on my way."

"Oh, I get it." She laughed. "Had to get gussied up for your hot date."

"We're taking Jay to the carnival. It's hardly—"

"See you in a bit." She ended the call.

~ ~ ~ ~ ~

Ivan pulled into Tucker's driveway, wondering if maybe he should park on the street. He didn't see Tucker's car, so maybe it was parked in the garage. Before he could decide, a car pulled in behind him. He glanced in his review mirror to see it was Tucker.

He took a deep breath, then checked his hair and teeth in the mirror. He reached down to unfasten his seatbelt and grabbed his phone, wallet, and sweater off the passenger seat, then exited the vehicle. Tucker was already there, standing right next to him.

"Do you need me to move my car?"

"It's fine right here." Tucker leaned in to him and kissed him softly on the lips. He held Ivan's shoulders with both hands. "And you're fine right *here*."

Ivan wondered for a second about Tucker's neighbors. It wasn't as if he lived in a secluded neighborhood. Anyone could be looking out their window or driving by. The possibility didn't seem to concern Tucker, so why should Ivan worry about it? God, the man smelled good.

"You taste like Tic Tacs."

Tucker reached into his pocket and removed a hand-held plastic dispenser. "Want one?"

"No, I'm fine. Already got the taste in my mouth." He grinned, and Tucker smiled in return. "Do we have to go pick up Jaydin?"

"He's in the backseat."

"Oh." Ivan glanced over to the car. "What if he just saw us…you know…"

"He already saw us kissing the other night. He was peeking out the door when I walked you to your car."

"Uh oh."

"It's okay. He's seen his mommy kiss other guys too."

"What if he outs your or something? I mean, what about your job?"

"I'm not worried about my job. I'm much more concerned about my son. I don't want him growing up believing it is somehow wrong or shameful for two men to kiss."

Ivan looked him right in the eye, a warm feeling sweeping over him. Maybe this guy really was a knight in shining armor. It was beginning to seem like he was too good to be true. "Wow.

You really are a good father." He had to look away or he'd start tearing up. He took a step toward Tucker's vehicle.

"We can take your car, if you'd rather," Tucker said. "Yours is much nicer."

"Your car is fine. It was nice enough for me to ride in for almost five hours on Saturday."

"I'm a detective, but in reality that's just a glorified cop. Police officers don't make big salaries...not like in the medical profession."

Ivan laughed. "You're not trying to pick a fight, are you? Or make me feel guilty?"

Tucker raised both hands. "Neither. Just explaining why I drive around in a ten year old car."

"Why doesn't the department provide you a vehicle?"

"They do. This is it."

Shocked, Ivan assessed him to see if maybe he was joking, but Tucker wasn't smiling. "I don't care how much money you make or what kind of car you drive." He continued toward the passenger door and opened it, leaning in to say hi to Jaydin before he slid into the seat. "Hey, big guy. Ready for some rides?"

"Yes!" Jaydin sat in the rear passenger seat, in a booster safety chair. "And I want cotton candy!"

Tucker opened his door and slid behind the wheel as Ivan climbed in. He fastened his seatbelt and continued his conversation with Jaydin. "Is that your favorite? Mine's caramel apples."

"Daddy, I want a caramel apple, too!"

Tucker turned to Ivan to offer a reproving look. "Weren't you the one saying I needed to do better with Jaydin's food choices."

"This is a special occasion, right Jay-Jay? You *have* to have cotton candy and caramel apples at the fair."

"It's not the fair, Ivan. It's the carnival."

"The carnival is like the fair sort of," Tucker explained. "They just don't have all the farm animals and stuff."

"Farm animals?" Jaydin laughed. "They have chickens?"

"And pigs, and sheep, and cows," Ivan said. "Kids like you raise the animals and bring them to the fair to sell them. And they get prizes for the best ones and wins ribbons."

"I want a cow!"

Tucker glanced at Ivan as Ivan concealed the big grin on his face. "Thanks a lot." He turned slightly to his son. "No, Bubby, no farm animals in town. We don't have room for a cow here...or at your mama's house."

Tucker backed the car out of the drive, and as he drove toward the business district of town, Jaydin kept chattering, going on and on about the different animals he knew. "We have bunnies at school," he said proudly. "And Ms. Anderson said they might have babies, but they didn't."

"They still might." Ivan spoke optimistically, adding a cheerful lilt to his voice.

"No, she said she was wrong. They can't have baby bunnies cause Fred and Frieda are both boy rabbits. She thought Frieda was a girl rabbit, so that's why she thought they could have babies. Boys can't have babies. Only girls."

Ivan gulped. "And do you still call her Frieda. Isn't that a girl's name?"

"Ms. Anderson said we can change Frieda to a boy name if we want, but nobody wants to. I don't think Frieda wants her name changed."

"You mean 'him'," Tucker corrected. "Frieda's a boy, right?"

"Not to me. She likes being a girl. She can't help it if she can't have babies."

"Oh…um…okay." Tucker turned quickly to Ivan, obviously now in unfamiliar territory. He didn't seem to know how to respond.

"Daddy, why can't boys have babies too?"

Tucker gulped and gripped the steering wheel tightly with both hands, staring straight ahead at the road.

"Do you think two boy rabbits would be good parents to baby bunnies?" Ivan asked.

"Yes. They would be two daddies, and daddies are good just like mommies are good."

"And that's all that matters, right? If both daddy rabbits love the baby bunnies, they can be a happy family."

"That's what I told Ms. Anderson, but she don't believe me."

"Look! I can see the Ferris Wheel." Tucker pointed through the windshield.

"Yay! I want to go on the Ferris Wheel. Please, Daddy!"

Ivan could read the relief on Tucker's face, probably at the subject change. "Let's get a parking place first, and then we'll go get our tickets."

~ ~ ~ ~ ~

Tucker stood by the fence, waiting alongside a group of other parents as they watched their little ones float by overhead, each housed safely inside an oversized bumble bee. Most of the kiddie rides were similar, featuring different themes, yet the rides themselves simply involved riding in some sort of car that gently careened up-and-down while rotating around the ride's core. This particular ride had cars that were designed like smiley-faced yellow jackets, hence it was called Bees. So far Jaydin had also ridden the Elephants, Monkeys, Dinosaurs, and Puppies. Tucker and Ivan had been taking turns accompanying him, and Tucker suspected he'd soon have to put the brakes on his little boy's fun. Jaydin wasn't about to wear out, and if he had his way, they'd be there all night going on the same rides multiple times.

He watched the bees overhead, and when Jaydin's approached he waved. Jaydin squealed excitedly and began to frantically wave in response. Ivan, sitting beside him, could not be all too comfortable in the tiny car, but he had his arm around Jay-Jay and was smiling. He waved as well, and in spite of himself, Tucker beamed from ear to ear.

What a bizarre first date, if that even was what you'd call it. How many guys would be like Ivan, so understanding and so eager to participate? He didn't seem to be faking it either. If felt as if he was loving every minute.

When the ride stopped and the passengers finally disembarked, Jaydin ran hurriedly across the lawn to his father. "I saw you Daddy!"

"I know. I was waving at you."

"I want to do the hot rod cars!"

"Really?" Tucker laughed and looked up at Ivan who had joined them beside the fence. "What are the hot rod cars?"

"Oh, the hot rod cars!" Ivan exclaimed. "Remember bumper cars?"

"Oh no. No bumper cars." Tucker shook his head emphatically. "When you get bigger —"

"No," Ivan interrupted. "Look, over there. In the kiddie rides they're different. I guess it's called Speedway, but it's sort of like bumper cars but the cars don't slam into each other."

Tucker stared at the ride, assessing it. "You and me ain't fitting into one of those cars." He laughed.

Ivan squatted down to face Jaydin at eye-level. "You can go on it, but you have to ride by yourself. Daddy and me are too big."

"Oh." Jaydin bit his lip as he thought for a minute. "I wanna do it! I can drive it myself."

"How about we get a hot dog or something? Aren't you hungry?" Jaydin didn't yet have much of an attention span. Maybe he could distract him.

"No, I want to do the hot rods! Please."

Tucker nodded. "Okay. We'll do the hot rods and then we're going to eat, okay?"

"And get cotton candy?"

"You already had cotton candy." Ivan laughed. "I see how you are. You're trying to trick Dad into getting you more cotton candy."

"But I only had the blue kind. I want pink."

"Come on." Ivan grabbed his hand. "Let's go get in line at the hot rods."

A few minutes later, when Jaydin ran out to get into his own car, Tucker and Ivan stood watching intently. Cripes, why'd he feel like he was sending his kid off to college instead of just a carnival ride. "Careful!" Tucker shouted, as Jaydin hesitated while getting in his seat. For a second he thought he was going to fall in.

When he felt a hand against his back, he looked over to Ivan who stood smiling warmly. "He's okay. He's right here in front of us, and we'll be able to see him the whole time."

"I know." Tucker cleared his throat. "Am I that obvious? I'm one of those parents, aren't I?"

"The overprotective kind?" Ivan nodded. "But not too protective to let go when you need to. Jaydin's lucky to have a dad like you."

God how he wanted to lean in right then and kiss him. Instead, he shifted slightly, then reached down to grab Ivan's hand. He squeezed affectionately and stared into his eyes. "And I'm lucky to have met someone like you. I just wish the circumstances had been different."

"Maybe it was fate. It's horrible what happened to my mom, but I know you're the right person to handle the case. You didn't railroad my father, but you actually investigated and accepted the evidence that you discovered. And I know you won't stop until you find the real killer. So yeah, I don't particularly like the circumstances that brought us together, but I'm glad you're in the position you are…and that I'm in the position I am right beside you."

Tucker squeezed Ivan's hand once more then looked out at the cars. They weren't traveling in all different directions, crashing into one another like the bumper cars. Instead they each traveled around the track in succession. Every car had its own steering wheel and horn, but the steering wheels didn't really control anything. The horns actually honked, though, and Jaydin wasn't holding back. He laid into it. *Beep! Beep! Beep!* He waved and giggled as he spotted them, and Tucker and Ivan each raised their hand, waving back.

After the hot rods, they found a booth selling hot dogs. Jaydin wanted a corn dog, which Tucker knew he wouldn't even eat half of. He'd finish what Jaydin didn't eat. They also got fries to share and soft drinks. Tucker remembered to order Ivan a diet.

"Oh. My. God." Ivan looked up from his seat at the picnic table. "Elephant ears." He pointed to the vending trailer on the other side of the walkway. "I have to…"

"Sit!" Tucker laid his hand on Ivan's shoulder, holding him down. "I'll get it."

"No, no…I can…" He looked into Tucker's face. Reaching up with one finger, he wiped the corner of Tucker's mouth. "You got ketchup—"

Tucker wrapped his lips around Ivan's finger and licked it off.

Jaydin laughed, holding out his own index finger which he'd dipped in ketchup. "Daddy, here. Eat this ketchup too." Tucker leaned down, grinning, and sucked the ketchup off his giggling son's finger.

"Let's eat our hot dogs first," Ivan said. "Then elephant ears!"

"Are they really elephants' ears?" Jaydin's eyes grew wide.

"No, honey." Tucker laughed. "They just call them that 'cause they're big and flat. The *look* sort of like elephants' ears."

"I don't ever want to eat a real elephant's ear." Jaydin made a face.

They continued devouring their carnival food and moved on to the elephant ear booth where they ordered a big one with cinnamon and sugar and all shared as they stood in line at the Ferris Wheel. Jaydin stood between them, holding his daddy's hand, and when Tucker looked down, his little man yawned. Tucker smiled, then scooped him up with one arm, holding him close.

Ivan smiled as Jaydin pressed his face against his daddy's shoulder. When they got to the front of the line, Ivan handed over the tickets and they climbed aboard. Jaydin roused a bit, looking around. Tucker placed the little guy between Ivan and himself and pulled down the bar. He stretched his arm across the back of the seat, behind Jaydin and Tucker, and allowed his fingers to brush against Ivan's shoulder.

As the ride began, Jaydin yawned again, and as his eyelids grew heavier, they began to close. By the time they reached the top of the ride, he was out.

"Thank you," Ivan whispered.

"For what?" Tucker couldn't seem to stop smiling. It had been so long since he'd felt this content. An inexplicable warmth spread within his chest.

"For including me in this. I've really enjoyed it."

"I want to take you on a real date — just you and me."

"To me, this is as real as it gets, but yeah, I'd like that."

~ ~ ~ ~ ~

"You could stay over if you'd like."

They sat cuddled together on Tucker's sofa. Jaydin slept soundly in his bedroom, all tucked in with his Pooh bear. Ivan framed Tucker's face with the palms of his hands and kissed him. He wanted to stay, oh God, did he ever. But it probably wasn't the best idea. They shouldn't spend their first overnight together with Tucker's four-year-old son in the next room. And Ivan had to deal with his father in the morning. He'd be returning from Florida.

"I want to. Really, I do, but…"

"It's okay. I understand." Tucker pulled him close. "Why don't you come over on Sunday for a cookout? It might be weird, though."

"What do you mean?"

"Janelle will be here, but she likes you. A lot."

"Really?" Ivan laughed softly. "Yeah, you're right. That might be kind of awkward."

"She's picking Jay up a day early. Normally I'd have him until Monday, but he's got a doctor's appointment so he won't be going to daycare on Monday."

"You don't go to his doctor's appointments?"

"Usually, but this is just a routine follow-up. It's just that it was easier for her to get the day off work this time."

"Well, I start back on day shift Monday morning. Sunday might not be the best time for a sleepover."

"It's up to you. If you want to come for the barbecue, we can see how it goes. If you want to stay over, fine. If not…another time."

Ivan ran his fingertips down the center of Tucker's chest. He'd love to get that shirt off him and curl up next to that hard, muscular torso. "I'll come early, help with food prep."

"Really?"

"Yeah." He found one of Tucker's nipples through the fabric of his form-fitting t-shirt. He rubbed it and gently squeezed. "Need me to bring anything?"

After a quick intake of breath, Tucker grinned. "Anything you want, but don't worry about the meat. I can provide *that*."

"Oh, I know. I've seen your big package of meat…even tasted it."

"Ivan, if you don't go now…"

"I know, it'll be too late." God, he wanted to peel that shirt right over his head and suck on those hard nipples.

Suddenly Tucker jolted, thrusting himself up from the couch. "Jaydin!" That's when Ivan heard it—the wheezing. It sounded like a freight train. Tucker rushed across the room and snatched Jaydin's backpack from the bureau. "He's having an asthma attack."

Ivan sprung from his seat into action, racing down the hall toward Jaydin's room. When he pushed the door open, Jaydin stood beside his bed, gasping, clutching himself as he tried to breathe.

"Do you have an inhaler?" Ivan shouted, but Tucker was already there. He hurried past Ivan and slid to his knees, wrapping an arm around Jaydin's shoulder. The little boy, terrified, stared into his father's eyes. Nothing was scarier than not being able to breathe.

Ivan lowered himself and took the inhaler from Tucker's trembling hand. He expertly attached the extension and held the device to little Jay's mouth. "Open. Come on, baby, open for me. There…there you go. Now when I say breathe, try really hard to take a breath. One, two, three, breathe." He depressed the trigger on the inhaler and Jaydin sucked in a draught of the medicine.

The vapor from the short-acting reliever traveled quickly to his lungs, relaxing the muscles of his airways. He continued to gasp for a couple seconds and then, still trembling, began to take more normal breaths.

"Do you have another inhaler?"

Tucker nodded. "We have to wait."

"I know. I'll go got it, though. Stay with Jaydin. Is it in the backpack?"

"Yeah. You're okay, honey." He rubbed Jaydin's back. "Daddy's here, just try to relax. Breathe nice and steady, in and out."

Ivan rushed back out into the living room. Chronic bronchial asthma attacks were an unfortunate reality for many children Jaydin's age. They were often brought on by excitement, and Jaydin had had plenty that evening. He'd be okay, though. He'd responded perfectly to the relief inhaler and probably wouldn't need to go to the ER for a nebulizer treatment. They'd wait a bit and then give him a dose from his regular, daily inhaler.

Father and son were sitting on the twin bed when Ivan arrived with the medicine. "You want to sleep with Daddy tonight?"

The teary-eyed little angel looked up into his father's face and nodded. Ivan's heart melted. He knelt down in front of them, handing Tucker the inhaler.

"Ivan, thank you…thank you so much. I…" He shook his head. "I'm not sure I'll ever get used to this."

"You did fine. You're *doing* fine." He looked at Jaydin, placing his fingertips gently under his chin. "And so are you. You want a drink of water?"

Jaydin nodded, and Ivan smiled. "He's okay, I think, ready for his inhaler. You want to do it?"

"Yeah." Tucker held the device up to Jaydin's mouth. "He's still learning exactly when to breathe. This one's a little trickier because it doesn't have the extension."

Ivan nodded. He was familiar with the complications of inhalers, how they were often challenging to small children. And when they were panicked, in the middle of an attack, it often was even more difficult. If the patient didn't breathe in at exactly the right second, the medicine would expel but not make it into the lungs.

He watched as Tucker administered the medication, doing so flawlessly. "Cool. Good job!" Ivan patted Jaydin's knee. "Be right back with your water."

When Ivan made it back a couple minutes later from the kitchen, Jaydin was already back in bed. His father lay curled beside him, spooning him. Ivan tiptoed into the room and set the glass on the bedside stand.

"I'll let myself out," he whispered. "Call me if you need anything." He raised his extended thumb and pinky to the side of his face.

"Thank you," Tucker mouthed.

Ivan slipped out of the room, and after a couple steps down the hall, stopped and leaned against the wall. He held both hands to his chest, clasping them together, and took a deep breath. "I'm falling," he whispered to himself. "I'm falling so fast."

Chapter Fifteen

"You wanted to see me?" Tucker stood in the doorway of his boss's office. She looked up from her computer.

"Brown, come in. Close the door." She motioned for him to have a seat.

"What's up?" He tried to sound casual as he slid into the chair, bracing himself for what he was sure would be the ass-reaming of his life.

She peeled off her glasses and placed them on the desk, then looked directly at Tucker. "Wanted to check with you on the Ramsey case. Any leads?"

"Actually…" He took a deep breath. This was it, the moment he'd been waiting for. He needed to come clean, explain to his boss that his personal life and the case had intersected, that there was now a conflict of interest. He needed to tell her that she should remove him from the case. Instead of recusing himself, though, he conveniently omitted the details about Ivan. "It's going great. I have a very solid lead, and I expect to wrap it up real soon."

"Um hmm." She stared at him skeptically. "So what is it you're not telling me?"

He shrugged and offered his sincerest expression of wide-eyed innocence.

"I know you, Tucker. Spill."

He sighed, defeated. There was no way out at this point without flat-out lying. "We hit a roadblock. All my key suspects had iron-clad alibis, or so it seemed."

"And…"

"And with quite a bit of digging, I think I've cracked it. Or, I should say, *we've* cracked it. Viviano has been working the case as hard as I have. We should have enough evidence to request a warrant by Monday, and then we'll turn everything over to the prosecutor."

"Who's your suspect?"

"The husband."

"Really? I thought he was checked into a motel over in Deckerville for the night."

"He was, but he left his room around 1:30. He used his girlfriend's car and dressed in disguise. But I got video from the toll booth security camera — clear shot of his face. Also have video of him on his way back to the motel two-and-a-half hours later. Don't know what he did with the weapon, but the ballistics match one of the missing handguns from his collection. He had motive — a half a million bucks in insurance and a girlfriend."

"We charging her as an accessory?"

"That'll be up to the prosecutor. Haven't even questioned her yet. Don't need to."

"Why wait 'til Monday? Go get him now."

Technically, Tucker wasn't even working. He and Jay had stopped in to the precinct and Jay was in one of the conference rooms with a uniformed officer, one of Tucker's friends. Tucker cleared his throat. "I'd like to wait, if you don't mind. The suspect's actually not even here, but will be returning from Florida in a couple hours. The flight arrives at 11:35."

"If you have the evidence you say you do, I want him brought in today. Go wait for him at the gate and make your arrest."

"Uh…"

"I don't see what the problem is. Oh…you were with your son. I forgot, this was your weekend. What the fuck are you doing in here on Saturday?"

"I had to stop in for some paperwork on another case. When I got here, I saw the message to see you."

"Ahh…okay, I get it. It's no big deal. I'll have Viviano make the arrest. I'll send another officer with him."

"No!"

Startled, she leaned back in her chair. "Tucker, what's going on? What are you not telling me?"

"It's just…I want to make this arrest myself. I'm kind of invested in this case, and to be honest, I could use a couple more days. I need to get my report together before I present everything to the prosecutor."

"Well, you can do that while the perp's in jail."

If Tucker made the arrest without warning Ivan, this could ruin everything. He'd be devastated and furious with Tucker for not telling him. Yet, he couldn't reveal details of the investigation. This was why they called it a conflict of interest.

"I know, I know, but please…please can you give me the time? Just two days. I guarantee he's not a flight risk."

"The man's a murderer. How can you guarantee something like that? He killed his own wife, and we have no idea who else he might target."

"Monday…I promise. Please, Briana. I'm still waiting on forensics with a couple things, and I have to get a video from Home Depot. Ramsey made a large purchase the day before the shooting. I believe he purchased items he used in commission of the crime."

With elbows on her desktop, she steepled her fingers together. "Alright, but only because you've never given me a reason not to trust you. I want an arrest made by Tuesday.

That'll give you time to get your evidence and your video." She pushed herself up from her seat. "Maybe then you can tell me what it is you're not saying. Now let me see that little angel of yours."

"Thanks, Bri. Thanks so much." He heaved a sigh of relief as he rose from his seat. "He's with Laura in the conference room. They're playing dinosaurs, I think."

~ ~ ~ ~ ~

Ivan waited anxiously by the baggage claim. His father's flight had landed already, so he should be arriving at any moment. Ivan spoke to him on the phone the night before, but only briefly. He promised to pick his dad up from the airport. Though their conversation had been cordial, it wasn't exactly what he'd consider warm. Businesslike — just like his father.

His dad had made no mention of a traveling companion. Diane Seavers had either made other transportation arrangements from the airport, or perhaps she hadn't come back with him. Maybe she'd already arrived on an earlier flight, for all Ivan knew. He didn't know the woman, not even what she looked like. He tried finding her on Facebook, but there were about a thousand users with that name. He hadn't pursued it very aggressively. He didn't really want to know.

But he did know that his father and he were going to have to have a very serious talk. Brandon had refused to even come to the airport, and Ivan had to first explain that. And he had to inform his dad that he wasn't welcome at Brandon's house anymore. Though it wasn't exactly fair that Ivan was the one stuck telling his dad, his brother and he both agreed it would be best. Brandon was still very angry about the cheating, and Ivan didn't blame him. Well, more accurately, he was hurt.

Ivan was hurt.

He hurt for his mother. Not only was she cheated out of God-only-knew how many years of life, but she'd also been the victim of her husband's deception and infidelity. Her church had been everything to her, and she'd certainly roll over in her grave knowing her widower was already flaunting a love affair with another woman. Flaunting? Well, only time would tell. He'd made little effort to conceal his trip to Florida.

Ivan felt jittery inside, as if he'd just consumed a full pot of coffee on an empty stomach. He also battled waves of mild nausea. When he felt anxious, his body always did this to him. He rose from his seat and thrust his hands into his pockets, glancing around. He then spotted him. His father, alone, emerged from the hallway leading into baggage claim. Ivan took a few steps in his direction, stopped, then continued on. When his dad looked up to see him, Ivan waved and smiled. He met his dad halfway.

They embraced, but only briefly. "How was your flight?"

His dad shrugged. "Okay for coach, I guess."

"I see you got some sun."

"And some much-needed rest. It was a nice getaway." He looked around. "Brandon with you?"

"Uh, no. Just me." Ivan smiled. "Let's see if I can remember your bags."

"That looks like them right there." His father pointed to the turnstile, and Ivan stepped over and grabbed them.

"Just two?"

"Yup, here, let me get one…"

"I got em, Dad." He connected the two pieces of luggage together using the extension bar on the bigger suitcase. It was on wheels, very easy for Ivan to pull. "I'm in the parking garage. It's not a long walk. We can either hoof it or you can wait for me to pull around."

His dad waved his hand dismissively. "We'll walk. What the heck."

As a deacon in the church, Ivan's dad was not prone to cursing, and Ivan could count on one hand the number of times he'd heard his father swear. Though Ivan never doubted his father's religious conviction, it wasn't something he wore like Ivan's mother did. She, being as obsessed as she was with appearances, displayed her Christianity for the world to see. His dad kept his beliefs private, and as with almost everything in his life, was very reserved about sharing them.

They made it to the car and loaded the suitcases into the trunk. As Ivan pulled around to the parking structure exit, Ivan's father removed his wallet. "I got this, Dad," Ivan said, pulling up to the pay booth.

"No, here." He held out a twenty, waving it in Ivan's face. Ivan reluctantly took the money, inserted his ticket receipt into the reader and then fed the twenty into the bill reader. He handed back his father's change, seven bucks.

"Hm. Thirteen bucks an hour?"

His dad shrugged. "More or less standard for short-term. You should have just pulled up in front of baggage claim and waited in your car." This was why Ivan was trying to refuse his father's money. He insisted on paying for things but then complained about it afterward. With all the insurance money he'd just received — and the life insurance he was yet to receive — you'd think he wouldn't have to be quite so frugal.

Then again, he'd just laid out fifteen grand for a diamond.

"Dad, there's something I need to talk to you about. Can we maybe go somewhere?"

"Sure, or we can talk at Brandon's."

"No, I…um…I don't want to talk there. You hungry at all? We can stop for lunch, my treat."

"You decide, and no, I'll pay."

He pulled into an Applebees a few minutes later. They could probably get a booth that might allow them a bit more privacy. Ivan requested the hostess seat them in the corner if possible, and his father seemed unfazed by Ivan's concern with being overheard.

Once seated, his dad didn't wait for Ivan to bring up the issue he wanted to discuss. After the server had taken their orders, his dad confronted Ivan. "I think I know what this is about. I know you had lunch with your mother the day before she died."

A bit surprised, Ivan sat upright in his seat. "Yeah, I did."

"And I know what you talked about. Your mother called me."

"Really?" In order to keep his hand from trembling, he picked up his ice water and took a big drink. This didn't sound quite right. Ivan distinctly remembered his entire conversation with his mom, and he recalled how she'd insisted that he *not* come out to his father. "What did she say?"

"She said you were going through some…um…personal problems—questioning yourself and your…um…attraction to women."

"Well, not exactly…"

"Ivan, what you choose to do in your personal life is none of my business. Of course, you surely must know how your mother and I believe…how she *did* believe, and how I still do. God created man and woman."

"Wait, this is *not* what I wanted to talk to you about, but I'm glad to know how you feel."

"I don't love you any less, and neither did your mother. I just hope you can respect my beliefs. Don't throw this lifestyle in my face and expect me to accept it as normal."

What the holy fuck? Am I even hearing this?

"Dad, stop!" His mother's rejection had hurt—a lot—but he wasn't feeling wounded this time. He was enraged. "I don't *care* if you accept my identity as a gay man. To be honest, that's about the least of my worries right now. What I *do* care about is the affair you've been having with this woman—this Diane Seavers. And about the diamond ring you bought her when Mom was still alive!"

Ivan had never seen the color drain from a person's face as quickly as it did his father's in that moment. His dad stared at him, pursing his lips and clenching his jaw, but not immediately speaking.

"You want to lecture me about lifestyle choices? Why don't we talk for a minute about adultery?" Ivan pointed his finger angrily at his father. "Please Dad, tell me I'm mistaken. Tell me the ring was for Mom. Tell me this lady is just a friend, a business associate."

His dad took a deep breath, then folded his hands together on the table, almost as if praying. "She's actually a secretary at church, and yes, the ring was for her. I've been trying to figure out how I'd tell you and Brandon."

"Well, Brandon knows, and that's why I had to pick you up at the airport. You're not welcome in his home."

His father nodded. "I see."

The server arrived with their food. Ivan and his father remained silent, both staring down at the table in front of them. There was no fucking way Ivan could eat a single bite. When the waitress had left, Ivan looked up at his dad. "How could you?" His voice was barely a whisper. "How could you cheat on Mom like that?"

"I don't know, Ivan. It's something that just happened. Your mother and I fell out of love years ago, and when Diane was hired at the church—well, we got to know each other. Things just sort of clicked for us. We didn't plan this."

"Did Mom know?"

He shook his head. "I think she may have suspected, but it wasn't something we ever discussed. I was planning to file for divorce, but I never got up the nerve. I kept putting it off...Ivan, I didn't want to hurt her. I didn't want to hurt anyone."

Ivan looked away, his eyes now moist. He couldn't help but shake his head. "How convenient for you. Now you don't *have* to tell her. She's gone."

"That's not fair." He reached across the table for Ivan's wrist, but Ivan pulled away from him. "You have no idea the guilt I've suffered."

At this, Ivan guffawed. "Suffered? You can't be fucking serious!"

Hid dad hung his head, not bothering to respond.

"And you took this woman with you to yours and Mom's place in Florida. Doesn't seem to me you've been suffering a whole lot lately."

The expression on his father's face grew sterner as he looked up into Ivan's eyes. "I won't be judged by you—of all people. I'm sorry my marriage to your mother wasn't the bed or roses you and Brandon always imagined it to be, but your mother and I were very cautious about not exposing you to our problems. A lot of the reason we stayed together for so long was you two. We didn't want to hurt either of you boys, and this is the thanks I get.

"You disgust me, Ivan. You know better than this. We didn't raise you to be this way. As horrible as your mother's untimely death was, it might actually be a blessing in disguise, because knowing her own son had chosen to be a *faggot* would have likely killed her eventually."

The blow of his father's harsh words hit him like a sledgehammer. Ivan's mouth dropped open, and he reached up to rub his jaw. It felt as if he'd just been struck.

"I'm not hungry any more. Can we go?"

"I'll get my luggage from your trunk and call a cab."

Ivan took one more sip from his water. "Fine." He slid out of the booth, spun around, and walked briskly to the door.

Chapter Sixteen

As Ivan left his father standing on the curb in front of the restaurant with suitcases in tow, he knew exactly where he should go. It only made sense for him to head over to Brandon's and tell his brother what had happened. He didn't go there, though. His car seemed to almost be on auto-pilot steering him to the only person he wanted to see at that moment.

He pulled into Tucker's drive, relieved to see his car in the garage, which happened to be open. He must have just gotten home from somewhere, or perhaps he had it open for some other reason — maybe was mowing the lawn or cleaning out the garage itself. He got out of his car and headed briskly across the sidewalk toward the front door, the one Tucker always used, but then stopped mid-step when he heard his name.

"Ivan!" It was Tucker. He emerged from the garage, smiling. He took one look at Ivan's face, and his smile evaporated. He moved quickly forward. "What's wrong?"

"Tucker!" He rushed toward him, collapsing in his arms and released a sob. Trembling, he sank into the embrace as Tucker wrapped his strong arms around him and held him close.

"Come inside," he whispered. "Come on."

With his arm around Ivan's shoulder, he guided him through the garage into the house. No sooner did they cross the threshold than another smiling face appeared. "Ivan!" Jaydin rushed up to him, but like his father, the little boy instantly detected Ivan's distress. "Why are you sad?"

Ivan knelt down and hugged the little guy. "I'm okay...now. Now that I'm here with you." He pulled back, smiling.

"We can color if you want."

Ivan nodded. "Maybe in a little bit. I need to talk to Daddy for a while first, okay?"

"Baby, why don't you go back to watching your cartoons for a few more minutes while Ivan and me talk about grown-up stuff? Then we can make lunch together."

"But Ivan's sad…"

"I know. That's why we need to talk."

His bottom lip protruded just slightly. "I want chicken nuggets."

"Deal." Tucker reached down to ruffle his son's hair. Jaydin headed back to the living room while Tucker and Ivan stepped into the kitchen. Once around the corner, Tucker pulled Ivan into his arms again and kissed him tenderly on the lips. "Baby, what happened?"

"I…" Ivan stepped back, shaking his arms, then finally reached up to wipe tears from his cheeks. "I just got back from the airport. I picked up my dad."

"Oh no."

"Needless to say, it didn't go well."

"Sit down." He guided Ivan over to one of the barstool type chairs at the counter. "Did you confront him about —"

"The affair? Yes. I did confront him, but only after he confronted me about my perverted homosexual lifestyle."

"So he somehow found out that you're gay?"

Ivan nodded. "He said Mom told him the night before she died. She apparently called him, which seems very odd to me. Tucker, she begged me not to tell my dad."

"Maybe she wanted to be the one to tell him."

"I guess so. But…" He took a deep breath.

"Want some water?"

He shook his head. "No. Sorry, I'm okay." He composed himself before continuing. "That's not the worst part. I just can't believe the horrible things he said to me. Tucker, he said…I don't even know if I can repeat it."

"You don't have to." Tucker took his hand.

"No, I want to tell you." He plowed forward, forcing himself to just spit it out — get it over like ripping off a Band Aid. "He said it was probably a blessing Mom died because it would eventually kill her just knowing her son was a faggot."

"Oh Ivan."

He was crying again, and Tucker rose from his chair and stood beside him, again pulling him into an embrace. "That's bullshit, and you know it."

"And he admitted to the affair, to buying the diamond, to the trip with his girlfriend."

"I'm so sorry he did this to you." Tucker's response was so different than Ivan would have expected. A few days ago, he'd have predicted that Tucker would respond to this sort of thing with anger and outrage, but bless his heart, he seemed far more concerned with comforting Ivan. "Will you stay here with us for the rest of the weekend?"

Ivan pulled back from Tucker to look him in the eye. "Really?"

Tucker nodded. "No pressure. Just relax and hang out with Jay and me. Let's just spend the next thirty-six hours, or whatever, not worrying about cheating, homophobic fathers or work or unsolved cases…"

"Just the three of us."

"And at times, when we can get away with it, just the two of us." He leaned in for a kiss.

Ivan wrapped his hands around the back of Tucker's head as they tasted each other, closing his eyes and savoring the moment. "Maybe a knight in shining armor's not such a bad thing, after all."

"Huh?"

"Nothing." Ivan laughed softly.

"I feel like *you're* the one who's been my knight in shining armor." Tucker sounded so sincere. "You've changed my life, even in this short time."

"Before we've even been on an official date?"

"We can remedy that...soon."

"I don't need a real date. I just need to be with you."

Their lips found each other again, and Tucker reached up, gently brushing tears from Ivan's cheeks. The kisses were tender and loving, and Ivan felt a warmth growing within his chest—the opposite of the emptiness he'd felt so many times since his mother's passing.

"That's what I told Ms. Anderson!" Ivan and Tucker pulled apart, both their heads turning quickly to the little man who'd just entered the kitchen. "I told her boys can kiss boys. And they can have babies too if they want to."

~ ~ ~ ~ ~

Ivan had lifted Jaydin up and placed him on the barstool next to him, and together they were coloring, jabbering away like no one's business. Tucker, who'd been putting groceries away when Ivan arrived, resumed the task. After he and Jaydin left the police station that morning, they went grocery shopping which happened to be one of Jay's favorite activities. Of course, he wanted everything he saw, most of which he'd have zero interest in eating once they got home. Shopping with a four-year-old was more like a game of distractions and selective hearing. If you couldn't distract him with a different item, you pretended not to hear. If that didn't work, you had to flat out say "No" — a couple hundred times.

"Hey!" Ivan hollered to Tucker. "How are we supposed to color here when we have no coloring music?" He turned on his stool, holding one hand to his hip in mock indignation.

"Coloring music?"

"I want coloring music!" Jaydin chimed in. "And dancing music, too."

Tucker laughed. "Shall I serenade you?"

"No, no…please." Ivan held up both hands in protest.

Tucker walked past them into the living room to his stereo system. He picked up his i-Pod and scrolled through his playlist until he came to the desired song. "I have a perfect coloring song for you," he hollered out to the kitchen. He made the selection and adjusted the volume.

As soon as the open strains of the electric guitars came through the surround-sound, Ivan cried out, "Oh yeah! Now you're talking." He sang along, word-for-word as the lyrics began. "I never meant to cause you any sorrow…"

Jaydin, excited, began to giggle and clap his hands.

"Purple rain, pur-ple rain…" Tucker sang along, probably at least a couple notes flat. He'd never been a great singer, but he loved his music, eighties and nineties rock his favorite. He sauntered back to the kitchen, stopping in the threshold and leaning against the frame. Tucker smiled as he watched Ivan hold his purple crayon in the air, swaying back and forth next to his son, singing every word.

As the song transitioned into the bridge, Ivan rose from his chair and slid, sock-footed across the kitchen floor, stopping in front of Tucker. Grabbing hold of him, he pulled him forward onto their makeshift dance floor and cuddled up to him, draping his arms around Tucker's neck as Tucker clung to Ivan's waist. They danced, swaying to the music, and Jaydin went nuts, applauding and cheering.

The lyrics of the song coursed through Tucker's soul as he held this amazing man in his arms. His heart swelled. Was this *it*? Was this what it felt like? He'd never felt such amazing warmth within himself and thrilled at every aspect of this incredible person who seemingly came from out of nowhere and filled his life with something Tucker couldn't quite describe — something that had been missing.

He leaned in, resting his face against the side of Ivan's head, inhaling his scent and basking in the warmth of his touch. As the song reached its crescendo and faded to its final, soulful strains, he hugged Ivan close. Closing his eyes briefly, he opened them and looked down when he felt small arms wrapped around his legs.

He pulled back slightly, leaning over, and scooped his little one up with one arm. Ivan grinned, leaning forward to kiss Jaydin softly on the forehead. "I guess we're not getting much coloring done, are we?"

"Coloring *and* dancing," Jaydin said. Ivan gave him a playful poke in the tummy.

"I guess we better get busy and get you some lunch before you starve, and then we can finish our pictures."

"Or we can dance and eat lunch for supper."

Ivan laughed. "Then what will we eat supper for?"

Jaydin thought for a second. "Breakfast!"

"You're silly." Tucker kissed the side of his head. He walked over to the barstool on which Jaydin had been sitting and redeposited his son. "You keep working on your picture, and we'll make lunch."

"I want—"

"Chicken nuggets," Tucker and Ivan said in unison.

~ ~ ~ ~ ~

After lunch, Tucker put Jaydin down for a nap while Ivan went outside and sat in one of the chairs on the porch. A dervish of conflicting emotions swirled within him—anger, hurt, fear. Intermingled with these harsh feelings were others, far more pleasant—passion, hope, and something that resembled love. This couldn't be love though, not yet. It was far too early, but it was something.

Was he grasping? He'd felt such grief and loneliness, perhaps the connection he was experiencing with Tucker was wishful thinking. He had a void within him, and it was due to the loss of his family. His mother had died, his father more or less disowned him, and the only person Ivan had left was his brother. But Brandon had already begun to forge a life of his own. He lived with Jessica, and they were happy. Ivan wanted that sort of happiness, that kind of security.

He leaned forward in his chair, resting his elbows on his knees, when the door opened and Tucker stepped out. Ivan looked up. "Is he sleeping?"

Tucker nodded. "Want to come inside for a minute? I want to show you something." He held out his hand. Ivan reached up and slid his hand into Tucker's as he rose from his seat. He allowed Tucker to lead him inside, across the living room, and down the hallway to a place in the house Ivan had yet to see—Tucker's bedroom.

As Ivan stepped across the threshold, Tucker pointed to the stand beside his bed. Ivan looked at it and then back at Tucker, confused. "You wanted to show me your intercom system."

"Well, it's a baby monitor."

"And…?" Ivan laughed.

"And Jaydin's sleeping. We have privacy finally, and we can hear in his room, if he happens to wake up." Tucker stepped over to the door and closed it. He looked back at Ivan and smiled. Then he locked the door.

"Even if Jaydin were to sneak out of bed—which he doesn't—he'd have to knock on the door."

A tinge of excitement raced through Ivan as a smile spread across his face. He moved quickly toward Tucker, grasping the bottom of his t-shirt and sliding it upward to expose his abs. "How do you find time to work out?" Ivan marveled at the cut, an eight-pack of solid muscle.

"After I drop Jaydin off at daycare, I have about an hour before work. That's my gym time. Or I go on the days he's at his mother's. But why are we talking about this?" He grabbed Ivan by the shoulders and planted a deep, passionate kiss.

Ivan gasped as he pulled back from the kiss. "I just wanted to know your secret. I had to make sure you were real and not some god hiding in a mortal's body."

"The other day, when you were on your knees worshiping me, you made me feel like a god."

"Good, cause I'm about to do it again." Ivan slid to his knees, fumbling for the button on Tucker's jeans.

Tucker peeled his shirt over his head, discarding it on the floor as Ivan splayed open his fly. He pressed his mouth against the bulge, allowing his hot breath to warm the already throbbing hardon. Opening his mouth, he lapped at the fabric of Tucker's underwear. Steadying himself, Tucker grasped Ivan's shoulders and moaned.

Unable to delay a second longer, Ivan took hold of the waistband of Tucker's briefs and slid them down. As Tucker's cock sprang forth, Ivan held it with one hand, pushing it back against Tucker's flat abdomen, and began to lick Tucker's balls.

"Oh Jesus fucking Christ!"

Encouraged by Tucker's enthusiastic response, Ivan continued licking, descending below the scrotum to lap at Tucker's taint. He stroked the shaft a bit as he kept teasing with his tongue, until Tucker's moans and exclamations at last convinced Ivan that Tucker'd been tortured enough. He rose up a bit and sucked the head of Tucker's cock into his mouth, staring upward at the flat plane rising to Tucker's rounding pectorals. Then Ivan sucked.

"Oh my God, baby…oh shit…you're gonna…I can't…aw fuck…"

Ivan pulled back, allowing Tucker's throbbing cock to bob in front of his face. He looked up from his kneeling position and smiled. "I want your big cock inside me," he whispered.

Without another word, Tucker leaned forward, sliding his hands beneath Ivan's arms and raised him to his feet. His lips crushed against Ivan's and his tongue unapologetically invaded his mouth. Ivan responded in kind, kissing and sucking passionately. Tucker held onto him and walked him the short distance to the queen-sized bed where he deposited Ivan on his back. Tucker pulled back and quickly finished tearing off his pants and throwing them into the pile with his discarded shirt.

Ivan began stripping off his shirt as Tucker unfastened the button on his pants and pulled them quickly down Ivan's legs. He pulled them completely off and threw them aside, then slid onto the bed, bracing himself with his arms against the mattress while covering Ivan with his body. Their hard cocks rubbed together, Tucker's still slick from Ivan's saliva. Ivan took Tucker's head in his hands and delivered a searing kiss as they humped against each other.

After a few moments, Tucker pulled away, gasping for air. He looked down into Ivan's eyes. "Baby, are you sure?"

"Positive," Ivan whispered.

Tucker leaned over and opened the drawer of the bedside stand. He removed a condom packet and some gel. First he handed the lube to Ivan, then used his teeth to tear off an edge of the condom wrapper. Ivan squeezed some of the liquid onto his fingers as Tucker rolled the condom onto his rock-hard shaft.

Now kneeling between Ivan's outstretched legs, Tucker reached down and cupped each of his palms beneath Ivan's thighs. Gently he raised them and then pushed back to spread them wide like a wishbone. Ivan reached down and applied the slippery gel to his hole as Tucker picked up the tube and squeezed some onto his sheathed cock. Once ready, he leaned forward again and kissed Ivan even more passionately than before.

As they were kissing, Tucker slid his hand down Ivan's body. Eventually his moist fingers found Ivan's lubricated hole. Slowly at first, he inserted one finger and began to frig. In and out. In and out. He pulled away from the kiss, staring into Ivan's eyes as he formed a small circle into Ivan's sphincter. Once the muscle had relaxed enough, he added a second finger.

"Oh God, that feels so good."

Tucker continued to fingerfuck him and intermittently planted sweet kisses on Ivan's lips, until at last Ivan could take no more. "Inside me!" he demanded. "Tucker, I need you inside me now!"

Tucker positioned himself directly between Ivan's legs and looked down at his cock. He grabbed hold of the shaft by the base and directed the bulbous head toward Ivan's welcoming hole. At first he pressed the spongy mushroom against his pucker, moving it slightly back and forth but not penetrating, then at last he eased forward. He allowed himself to sink in only a few centimeters, then stopped, gazing all the while into Ivan's eyes.

"You okay, baby?" He rubbed the fingertips of his free hand against Ivan's smooth chest.

"More," Ivan whispered.

He slid farther in. Ivan moaned. Farther still. At last he was balls-deep, impaling Ivan with his cock. "Oh shit...fuck me, Tucker. Oh God, please!"

Tucker began to rock back and forth, swiveling his hips as he pumped in and out. With each thrust, Ivan felt himself edging close and closer to orgasm. As Tucker pounded him, Ivan's prostate continued to be massaged, and Ivan knew his eruption was imminent. "Fuck, Tucker, you're gonna make me lose it. Oh God I'm so close!"

This only encouraged Tucker, whose torso now glistened with a sheen of sweat. He smiled down at Ivan and went for broke. "Oh God...oh yeah..." His face began to twist into an expression of ecstasy — or torture (Ivan couldn't tell which) at exactly the same moment Ivan felt himself cresting his own point of no return. He cried out as Tucker moaned, and ropes of cum fired from Ivan's hard cock onto his belly.

Trembling, Tucker blasted his load into the condom, and once spent, collapsed onto Ivan, crushing his lips once again with yet another fervent kiss.

Gasping, he pulled out of Ivan and rolled onto the mattress beside him. He disposed of the condom into the trash, and took Ivan's tear-streaked face into his hands and kissed him once more. "You're crying," Tucker whispered.

"I do that sometimes." He laughed softly. "I'm sorry, I don't know why — it's when I have a really intense orgasm."

Tucker pulled him against his naked body and Ivan laid his head onto Tucker's shoulder. "That was amazing." He reached up and gently raked his fingers across Tucker's perfect, muscular chest. "Absolutely amazing."

Chapter Seventeen

Tucker had never hosted an adult guest in his bedroom, not even when Jaydin was at his mom's. The idea of making love to another man while his son slept a few feet down the hall had made him squeamish, but there really was no logical reason for his discomfort. Didn't married couples do this all the time? Of course they did, or they'd never have more than one child. And straight people did it all the time, even if they weren't husband and wife.

Clearly Tucker still had issues with his sexuality he needed to work through. A lot of his trepidation and fear stemmed from stereotypes he'd learned from society. He'd picked up some of these negative attitudes, and often they were not even conscious thoughts. People assumed women were always better parents when it came to nurturing and looking after small children. They were better at comforting them, teaching them, clothing and bathing them…feeding them. Gay men were self-absorbed and shallow, and they were obsessed with sex. Men in general were impatient, dominant, and selfish.

Many of these stereotypes threatened Tucker's psyche, fighting to emerge from the back of his mind. They affected his confidence and his self-esteem. Add to that, his profession as a police detective carried another whole set of stereotypes, some of which he'd already addressed with Ivan.

There had to be a way to find balance, to blend his identity as a loving father with who he was as a gay man. Ivan seemed to be the puzzle piece that had been missing. Having him in the house, around Jaydin, partaking in their lives, felt right. It felt amazing, actually.

But how was Ivan going to feel when Tucker arrested his father? Granted, the man deserved everything that would be coming to him, but Ivan didn't. He'd just lost his mother, and now Tucker would be the one to snatch his only remaining parent from him. Once in custody, David Ramsey would not likely ever see the light of day again. Would Ivan be able to understand? Would he forgive Tucker for doing his job, or would he blame him?

"What are you thinking about?" Shirtless, and with a towel draped around his neck, Ivan slipped onto the sofa beside Tucker. They'd showered separately — just in case.

Tucker turned to him, smiling. "You."

"You're not feeling guilty are you?"

"God, no. For what?"

"Fucking me like a madman while your little boy lay sleeping down the hall," Ivan whispered, then giggled.

Tucker smiled again, perhaps more wanly this time. He raised his hand to his face, massaging his temples with his thumb and middle finger. He sighed and lowered his hand, staring into Ivan's eyes. "Actually, yes. I know it's stupid, but…"

"I understand." Ivan slid his hand onto Tucker's thigh. "But please just let me throw this out there. If you were straight and I was a woman, do you think you'd feel different?"

"Weird. It's like you're reading my mind. I was just thinking about all that. It really is a double standard. Why is it 'dirty' for gay men to make love? Why is it called 'sodomy'?"

"Because people are like my father. They're attached to a belief system that's very rigid, very exclusive. They're incapable of seeing love for what it is—colorblind, gender-blind. It's like my grandma used to tell me. Love will go where it's sent. And I was sent to you…and you to me." He leaned over and kissed

Tucker softly on the lips. Tucker rubbed his hand against Ivan's back, caressing his bare skin.

"You're beautiful, even with wet hair. *More* so with wet hair, I think." He grinned.

"You're pretty damn sexy yourself." Their gaze into each other's eyes lingered even longer than normal, until finally Ivan spoke. "I've been meaning to ask. Have you had any leads on the case?"

Tucker took a deep breath. *Shit, this is it.* "Babe, you know I'm not supposed to…"

"You're not supposed to talk about it, but you're also not supposed to be romantically involved…" He stopped midsentence. "Did I just say romantic?"

Tucker laughed. "I don't think there's any denying that we were just romantic with each other."

"True." Ivan nodded. "I understand what you're saying about being bound by confidentiality restraints, but you trusted me before. You even let me watch the video with you."

"I know." *I never should have breached protocol that way.* "I know I did, but maybe I shouldn't have. Ivan, you're right, I did trust you. Now I'm asking you to trust me. There are things I've discovered in the case." He swallowed hard. "New evidence, and it's all going to come to light very soon, but I can't talk about it. Can you please trust me to do what I'm required to do, and to apprehend your mother's killer?"

Ivan stared at him for a moment, then finally nodded. "Yes. Yes, I *can* trust you, Tucker Brown. Just like I know you'd trust me to do my job, even if it was as your son's nurse."

"I really would…and do." He kissed Ivan softly on the lips once more. "Thank you."

~ ~ ~ ~ ~

174

Jaydin's ninety minute nap had been a sweet little respite in Ivan's first day of real-life parenting. But when the little guy finally awoke, he was a ball of energy. Ivan loved children, particularly the young ones around Jaydin's age, but he normally dealt with them in a hospital setting, when they were sick.

Dealing with pre-school aged children required a level of patience that not every adult possessed. Kids that young usually didn't have really long attention spans. You had to keep them entertained, focused, and engaged. Otherwise, they'd be the ones vying for *your* attention.

Ivan loved watching Tucker interact with his son. Unlike a lot of single parents, he didn't just shove his little boy in front of a TV or computer screen. He actively participated in Jaydin's life, and he allowed his son to be a part of his own, adult life.

When Jaydin scurried into the dining room that evening while Ivan and Tucker were in the kitchen preparing supper, his dad looked up. "What ya got there, kiddo?"

"Leggos, Daddy." He expertly navigated the kitchen chair, climbing into the seat even while holding the large tub of plastic building blocks.

"We're going to be eating soon," Tucker reminded his son.

"I want to make a house," he announced.

"Can't it wait till after dinner?"

Ivan touched Tucker's arm, leaning in to whisper. "We have at least forty-five minutes to an hour before we eat."

"All right, but when it gets close to time to eat, you have to put all your Leggos away. Got it?"

"Okay, Daddy." And with that, Jaydin peeled off the lid of his Leggos container and dumped the entire contents into an enormous pile in front of him. Ivan stifled his laughter in response to the mini avalanche.

"Oh geez." Tucker shook his head.

"At least he's occupied." Ivan stepped over to the counter where the barstools were placed. He looked across, into the dining room. "Wow, that's a lot of Leggos."

"I need a lot to make a big house. Daddy needs to have a big, big house, even bigger than Mommy's so that you can come live with us."

Ivan spun around to glance at Tucker, wondering what kind of reaction he'd have to this announcement. Ivan couldn't help but laugh a little when he saw the flabbergasted expression on Tucker's face. "Honey, Ivan has his own place where he lives."

"I know, but I like him here with us."

"I like that too, but…"

"It's not a *real* house, Dad. It's for pretend, remember?"

Ivan moved closer to Tucker, sliding his hand around his waist. "It's for pretend, silly," he whispered, then stood on tiptoe to kiss him.

"Yeah, it might be pretend, but Jaydin's got a good point." He placed his hands on Ivan's waist. "It's really nice having you here. It's wonderful, really."

"I agree." He grinned as he pulled away and stepped over to the other counter. "Now get busy. That Parmesan's not going to grate itself."

"This is the second Saturday night in a row I've spent watching cartoons." Ivan scooped a fistful of popcorn into his mouth. The three of them sat on the couch, Jaydin in the middle with the bowl in his lap.

"You watched a kid's movie last week too?" Tucker had his arm draped across the back of the sofa and used his fingers to tickle Ivan's ear.

"I watched Moana last weekend over at my friend Carrie's. She has a little girl named Madison, a little older than Jaydin."

"I love Moana!" Jaydin said cheerfully. "Can we watch Moana next?"

"We're watching Dory right now, and that's enough." Tucker ruffled his son's hair. "And you've seen Moana at least five million times."

"A zillion! Is a zillion more than five million?"

"Slightly."

Ivan tucked his legs under himself, sitting like a pretzel. For some reason, he was comfortable watching television in this position. He reached over to grab more popcorn. "I like watching movies over and over," he confessed.

"My favorite movie to watch repeatedly when I was a kid was Charlie and the Chocolate Factory," Tucker confessed.

"I love that one, and of course, Wizard of Oz."

"I want to watch Wizard of Oz!"

"How about we all shut up and just watch *this* movie?" Tucker suggested.

"Sorry," Ivan mouthed, before devouring another handful of popcorn.

~ ~ ~ ~ ~

At last Jaydin was down for the night, and Tucker found himself again alone with Ivan. He wanted nothing more than to strip him naked and make love to him once more. Instead that sat on the porch, under the awning, sharing a bottle of wine.

"I probably shouldn't say this, but this reminds me of when Janelle and I first got married."

"*This* does?" Ivan made a gesture with his hand, fingers extended as he whirled it in a circular motion. "Why's that?"

"This is what we did every night...or a lot of nights. We didn't have Jaydin, but we didn't have much money, and I was too proud to ask my folks for help. Cripes, we didn't even have cable TV, but we had each other, and we'd sit out under the stars with a bottle of wine after working our asses off all day long."

"Your parents have been pretty supportive of you? You mentioned them before."

He nodded. "Not a lot of biracial families in their small Nebraska town...and even fewer gay couples. I'm the fulfillment of the deepest fears of half the parents in the state. The two things they're most terrified of hearing from their sons are 'I'm gay' and 'I'm marrying a black girl'."

"Tell me about them. What are they like?"

"Mom's an elementary school teacher. Dad was a foreman at a local factory until about ten years ago when they closed up and moved to Mexico. Now he's working for a renewable energy company, selling and installing solar panels."

"Wow."

"When I came out to them, Mom said she always knew. I told I wish she'd have let me know before I'd gone and married Janelle."

Ivan smiled.

"But like I said before, I ain't sorry. We've got Jay because of it."

"Would you think less of me if I told you how jealous I am of you?" Ivan squeezed his hand.

"I would think *less* of you, no. Might think you're crazy, but not less of you."

"Not in a green-with-envy kind of way. It's just I always imagined having that kind of unconditional support and love from my parents. In our house it was about maintaining appearances. For Brandon and me both. Of course, he's the epitome of the All-American son. But you know what's kind of weird? My parents believe very strongly in the Bible. They're...or I mean, they *were* when my mom was alive...evangelicals — born-again Christians. And they don't believe in any kind of sex outside of marriage. Yet they had very little problem with my brother living with his girlfriend. My mom said something about it once, how she wished they'd just get married. But ya know, it wasn't a big deal. And look at my dad. He's been carrying on this affair with another woman. He can somehow, in his own mind, justify his adultery, yet neither one of them could accept me...because I'm gay. They said it was a behavioral choice, a terrible sin." Ivan was beginning to choke up. "Why? Why is it more of a sin for me to be gay than for Brandon to live with his girlfriend? Why is it worse for me to love another man than it is for my dad to fuck some whore he met at church?" He was now whisper-shouting.

"Ivan, I'm sorry." Tucker wrapped his arm around his shoulder. They sat with their patio chairs side-by-side. "You're right. It's hypocrisy." *Did he just say 'love'?* "They're telling you that you're sinful because of who you are and saying you've chosen to be this way, yet in their own lives they make choices that by their own standards are clearly sinful."

"Yeah...and that's why I feel jealous. I just wish I'd have had a family that supported me like yours has. Actually, Brandon *has*, but not my parents."

"Maybe just try to focus on that one good thing. You have your brother, and that's more than a lot of gay people can say."

"True. He's an awesome brother. What about your siblings?"

"It's just me. Only child. I think that's part of the reason my parents were so happy when I got married. It was their one shot at grandkids. Guess they hit the jackpot."

"Yeah, they sure did."

Tucker to a sip of his wine. "You haven't seen all of me yet. You have yet to meet any of my friends."

"Hm. Well, I could say the same thing. You've met Dustin at the bar, or at least you saw me with him. And I know you talked to my friend Carrie. Those are the two people I'm closest to. I don't have a lot of gay friends, and it's not like we have this thriving gay community here. I have some friends from college I still keep in touch with online."

"I have my partner Martin. Goes by his last name, though— Viviano."

"Yeah, he's the one I talked to, the guy who gave me your business card."

"Couple other friends from the precinct. Laura, one of the uniformed officers, is gonna be here tomorrow at the barbecue, and hopefully Vivano. And of course, you know Janelle. She's my ex, but we're still close friends. To be honest, she's my best friend."

"She's to you who Carrie is to me."

"Sounds like it."

"Well…" Ivan slid his hand into Tucker's. "It doesn't sound like we have many surprises to reveal, not unless there is some deep, dark secret you're not telling me about."

Only that I'm about to throw your father in prison for the rest of his life. Tucker smiled, shaking his head.

"Then maybe you should take me back inside, to your bedroom, and make passionate love to me again."

"What if wanted *you* to make passionate love to me?" He delivered a tender kiss, grinning.

"Well, isn't it something we sort of have to do together?"

"What if I wanted you to fuck me this time?"

"Ahhh…I should've known a sexy guy like you would be versatile."

"Are you?"

"I'm very versatile. And you just made me hard as a rock." He grabbed Tucker's hand and pulled it into his lap.

"Mmm…let's go!" He leapt from his seat, grabbing hold of Ivan's wrist and dragged him inside, down the hall, and once in the bedroom, he locked the door. It remained locked for about an hour or so, until finally the couple emerged, one at a time, to each use the shower.

Tucker slept spooned around Ivan until the wee hours of the morning when another warm little body crawled into bed, wiggling his way in between them.

"Do you have to go potty?"

"I already went, Daddy." He yawned, still sleepy.

"Too early to get up. Go back to sleep a little longer."

Ivan rolled over, peeking through the slits of his eyes. "Is it morning already?"

"No!" Tucker protested. "Go back to sleep."

And together the three of them cuddled as they slept for the next two hours.

Chapter Eighteen

Tucker got his opportunity to showcase his pancake-making skills later that Sunday morning, and Ivan watched with amusement. One thing about the man was that when he was confident about something, he was *very* confident. He made Jaydin and Ivan each a huge Mickey-Mouse shaped pancake as big as the real Mickey Mouse's actual head.

It was after breakfast that Ivan's gay genes took over. "The dinner party guests are going to be here by four. We have a lot to do!" He whipped into motion, preparing a huge fruit salad and potato salad, and began gathering everything needed for the cookout.

"Ivan, it's not a dinner party. It's a barbecue."

"Same thing." Ivan waved his hand dismissively at Tucker. "You're having guests over to your home." Perhaps it was his mother's spirit invading his body, but he suddenly became focused on all the details. *Appearances matter.* He could almost hear his mother in his head. "I've got the kitchen under control, if you and Jaydin can tidy up the living room."

"Okay, okay, but I highly doubt we're going to be spending much time in the living room. We'll be outside mostly, in the back yard."

"Still, people are going to have to walk through the living room, right? Oh, and I better give the bathroom a once-over."

Janelle was the first to arrive a few minutes before four, and she brought with her a three-bean salad. Excited to see Ivan, she rushed up to him, depositing the bowl she was carrying on the kitchen counter, and hugged him ferociously. "I just *knew* it!" she exclaimed. "I told Tucker you and he batted for the same team."

"And now we all bat for another team. Team Jaydin."

"He adores you. He couldn't stop talking about you when I picked him up Wednesday." She paused and her smile faded a bit. "Honey, I'm so sorry about your mom." She touched his arm.

"Thank you." Ivan smiled sincerely. "That means a lot."

Tucker's partner, Viviano, was the next to arrive, and when he stepped through the door, Jaydin went racing across the room to greet him. "Uncle Marty! Uncle Marty!"

But when Tucker brought his partner into the kitchen to introduce him to Ivan, Viviano gave Tucker a strange look. Was it bewilderment? Of course, he had to have recognized Ivan. He was working with Tucker on the murder case, so he certainly remembered who Ivan was. He was very cordial, though, not mentioning so much as a word of the case.

"I go by Vivano...informally," he explained to Ivan. "Martin when I'm in trouble, and Marty when it's my mother. Uncle Marty to this one here." He pointed to Jaydin.

"Is this a cop thing?" Ivan laughed. "Last names are informal, and first names are formal."

"Pretty much." Tucker stepped over and slid his arm around Ivan's waist.

The other guest, Laura, showed up shortly after Viviano, and she brought her boyfriend. Had she not introduced him as Rich, Ivan wasn't sure he'd have been able to tell he was male. Prior to their introduction, Ivan had thought two women entered together, a lesbian couple perhaps. The one seemed a bit on the butch side. But Ivan figured it out rather quickly, particularly by the use of male pronouns.

He'd known a few transgender people while in college, but he hadn't met any in the Fulton area. It was kind of cool that a precinct of that size had at least one out gay man and one female cop who was dating a trans man.

The way everyone got along—chatting and joking with each other—amazed Ivan. He'd been to a lot of parties but couldn't remember any where everyone instantly clicked like this. Granted, it was a small gathering, but they all felt like family, and Ivan loved being in the thick of it.

Ivan had all the food prep completed, so when Tucker and Viviano announced they were ready to fire up the grills around four-thirty, Ivan directed them to the trays of marinating steaks in the refrigerator. "Oh dude, these look killer," Viviano said, slapping Ivan on the shoulder.

"Well, I can't take the credit. Tucker had already done the shopping yesterday before I got here."

"I just asked the butcher for a half dozen ribeye," Tucker explained. "Ivan did the rest."

The way Tucker's friends interacted with him, the way they accepted Ivan as part of the group, gave Ivan pause, and he recalled the conversations he'd had with Tucker about what Ivan thought of cops. Perhaps these friends didn't exactly represent a typical group of police officers, but they certainly proved Ivan wrong for having painted them all with a broad brush. Maybe there were some who were not authoritarian, who didn't see the world in hierarchal terms of black and white.

The steaks were amazing, and everyone raved about the dishes Ivan had thrown together. He wasn't sure how much of the compliments were just politeness. And the alcohol also played a role in how friendly they all were.

Around six-thirty, Janelle began taking inventory of Jaydin's things, gathering up his backpack and medicines. Tucker informed her of Jaydin's asthma attack the night of the carnival, and she thanked Ivan personally for being there to assist. The little one didn't want to leave and begged his mom to stay just a few minutes more. He was sitting on Uncle Marty's lap telling him all about the carnival rides. Finally she put her foot down and insisted it was almost bedtime.

Jaydin ran to Ivan, hugging him fiercely, and Ivan picked him up to give him a kiss on the cheek. "I love you, Ivan," Jaydin said into his ear, and Ivan all but choked up. He squeezed the adorable angel a little harder and kissed him again.

"I love you too."

Once Janelle and Jaydin had gone, that left Ivan with three cops and one aspiring law enforcement officer. Rich was currently in school studying criminal justice. As they continued to consume alcohol, the conversation became more about work, and after a bit, Ivan found himself sitting there not exactly knowing how to fit in.

He rose from his seat at the picnic table and went inside, not at all angry or hurt, just feeling a bit like a third wheel. He started to put things away and clean the kitchen when Tucker walked through the door. "Are you okay?"

Ivan looked up, smiling. "Yeah. I had a great time, and your friends…they're great."

"Did someone say something?" Tucker's expression was gravely serious.

"To me?" Ivan shook his head. "No, of course not."

"I just, um…I hope you're not upset about something."

"Not at all." He placed the dishrag he was holding in the sink and stepped over to Tucker, sliding into his arms. "You gave me an amazing weekend." He kissed Tucker on the lips. "But I probably should get going home. I have to work in the morning."

"You could stay over and leave from here."

"My work clothes are at home." He looked down at the shirt he was wearing, one Tucker had loaned him that morning. "Oh, and I'll just wash this and bring it back to you."

"Or you can keep it."

"Thank you again for being there for me. I think I really fell apart yesterday — overreacted to what my father said."

"You didn't, and I'm glad I was there for you."

"I'm going to just give him time. Maybe he'll come around eventually."

"You sure you don't want to stay." Tucker pulled him in close to his chest. "I really don't want you to go."

"I know, but I have to. And you guys...you're talking shop."

"We can talk about something else."

Ivan laughed. "No, you're fine. I have a long day tomorrow, twelve hour shift. If I stay, we'll be up half the night doing you-know-what."

"I do know what, and that's why I don't want you to leave." This time Tucker laughed. "Well, that's not the only reason. I love having you beside me, waking up next to you."

"With a rugrat in between us."

"Ivan, thank you so much. Thank you for..."

Ivan looked at him, and for the first time, saw Tucker's eyes turn glassy, possibly tearing up.

"Thank you for making my life better. I really...care about you."

"I care about you too." They kissed, slowly and deeply, then pulled apart. "I've got to go."

~ ~ ~ ~ ~

Although he didn't have to be to work until nine that morning, Ivan rolled out of bed a little after six. Memories of the weekend swirled in his head, and without question, the good far outweighed the bad. He'd been devastated by his father's cruelty, but being a part of Tucker's and Jaydin's life had more than made up for it. Everything just felt so right when he was with the man.

In so many ways, their pairing was a contradiction of what Ivan envisioned for his future. Yes, he'd always imagined being a father, having a family, but his dreams didn't quite match up with the reality that existed with Tucker. Physically, Tucker was everything Ivan could hope for — tall, broad shoulders, dark hair and eyes. He was the embodiment of the phrase "tall, dark, and handsome". And he was intelligent and most definitely well-read, but he wasn't refined. There wasn't a pretentious bone in the man's body.

Ivan had always kind of imagined himself meeting someone more artsy, someone who was more a member of the intelligentsia, an elite — someone who knew about interior design, art history, or how to throw a fabulous dinner party. Instead, Tucker knew how to fix a lawn mower or a carburetor. He knew how to handle a firearm, how to grill a steak on the barbecue. But Tucker also knew how to calm a little boy's fears after he'd had an asthma attack. He knew how to make Mickey-Mouse pancakes, for fuck's sake. And Goddamn did he ever know how to fuck.

Maybe this was the person Ivan had been looking for all along.

This battle raged within Ivan's soul. He'd spent the early part of his twenties trying to shed the puritanical hang-ups he'd learned from his mother. He told himself constantly that he didn't really believe that appearances were important. He cared about substance. He cared about what was in a person's heart, not about how they dressed and talked or how much money they made. But he had somehow managed to allow his mother's core beliefs to shape how he thought, subconsciously, if nothing else.

No, he really didn't need or necessarily even want a snooty, upper class man to share his life with. His parents had worked very hard to present themselves as upper middle class. Though his father's background was in hardware, he'd amassed a lot of money, and they were upstanding members of their church and of the business community. But look at their marriage. Look what a sham it was, the way appeared so perfect and so happy but had stayed together merely for the sake of appearances.

Before meeting Tucker, Ivan's life had been a series of loose ends. He'd completed a nursing degree and had a job that he loved, but beyond that, he had no idea where his life was going. His biggest challenge had been to find a way to come out to his family, and maybe then he'd be able to move on and begin getting serious about finding someone to settle down with.

Then along came Tucker. Now it felt strangely as if those loose ends had suddenly been tied off. In spite of the heartache and grief he felt over his parents, he looked toward the future and saw possibilities. He saw Sunday morning pancakes and carnival rides. He saw sneaking in some passionate lovemaking during naptime. He saw sharing bottles of cheap wine on the porch under the stars.

He almost picked up his phone to call Tucker, but then he remembered how early it was. He slipped on his workout clothes and headed to the community gym, a building on site at his apartment complex. It was free and had everything Ivan needed. Plus it was private, and at this time of the morning, he'd be the only one there.

He pushed himself hard, remembering the caramel apple, cotton candy, and ribeye steak he'd consumed over the weekend. When he got back to his apartment an hour later, he put on a pot of coffee and showered, then got dressed for work.

It was going to be a long day—a long three day stretch, actually. He wouldn't be off work until nine tonight, probably too late to see Tucker. But maybe he could call him. Or maybe Ivan would text him during the day while on lunch or break.

It felt amazing to be so giddy and excited about a man. He hadn't felt this way in years not since he first met Liam back during his freshman year. And God, this thing with Tucker was so much better than what he had with Liam. Even after only a few days, he knew Tucker was nothing like that phony. Tucker was a straight shooter, a very honest man, and Ivan was crazy about him.

He might even be more than crazy about him. He might even be starting to love the police detective.

Ivan's Monday proved more hectic than he had even imagined it might be. Day shift was always like this, and Monday's were the worst. He felt like he was on a dead run all morning, and by four o'clock in the afternoon, he realized he still hadn't taken a lunch. Starving, he got one of his coworkers to cover his rooms so he could squeeze in his break before the patients received their evening meals.

He stopped by his locker to pick up his cell phone before heading to the cafeteria. When he looked on his call log he realized he'd gotten five missed calls. Four were from Brandon, the other from Tucker. Rather than checking voicemail, he dialed his brother.

"Ivan, where the fuck are you?"

"I'm at work. I don't get off till nine."

"Have you been watching the news?"

"No, of course not." He leaned against his locker, annoyed. "Brandon, what's wrong."

"It's on the news. They cut in on the local station to announce the police had made an arrest in Mom's murder."

"What?" *Why on earth wouldn't Tucker have…wait, that must be why he called.* "Do they say who it is? Who'd they arrest?"

"Ivan, are you sitting down? I think you should be sitting—"

"Just fucking tell me!"

"They arrested Dad. That police officer, the one you said showed you the video clearing him…"

"Tucker."

"Yeah, well he apparently lied to you, because Dad's not clear. He's in fucking jail, and they've charged him with first degree murder."

Chapter Nineteen

After Ivan left the barbecue Sunday night, Viviano and Laura confronted him about his involvement with Ivan. He wasn't in the mood to receive criticism, though. "Ivan's the best thing that's ever happened to me, and Jaydin loves him."

"But, dude, you could lose your job — or be suspended and demoted," Vivano told him. "Why don't you just recuse yourself? Turn the case over to someone else."

"It's too late for that. If I drop the case now, I'll just be a quitter."

"Oh bullshit." Laura took a swig from her beer bottle. "You did the work. You cracked the case, which you're going to be turning over to the prosecutor anyway. What difference does it make if you hand it off to someone else to make the arrest?"

God, how did he end up in this predicament? He should have listened to Janelle the day after he kissed Ivan at the bar. She'd told him to resign from the case. Then again, had he taken her advice, he wouldn't have gone on the road trip with Ivan. They might have never connected.

Vivano, who was sitting across from him at the picnic table, leaned forward, elbows on the table. "Think about it, man. If you do make this arrest, Ivan's going to see you hauling his father away in handcuffs. Even if he's not there to watch it, there will be reporters present at the station. This is a high-profile case, and they're going to film it. He's going to see you on the news locking up his father."

"But this isn't even about Ivan's father. Our job is to enforce the law and see to it that justice is served. I'm doing this for Ivan's other parent — his mother, the crime victim."

Laura nodded, acknowledging his point. "And eventually Ivan will realize that, of course. He'll have to figure out, one way or another, how to reconcile his feelings for his father with the grief and outrage he feels on behalf of his mom. This won't likely happen overnight. He's going to be hurt. He's going to need someone to blame, someone besides his father. And it might be you. He might be so hurt by what he perceives as your dishonesty that he lashes out at you."

Like he did to his own brother, Brandon, when he delivered the evidence of their father's affair.

"You're right, so what do I do?"

"Go immediately to Bri in the morning. Tell her everything," Laura said. "Tell her about your involvement with Ivan. Don't sugarcoat anything, and take responsibility for your actions. She won't be happy. She's likely to be pissed that you kept this from her and compromised the case. But she's also human, and she really likes you." Laura smiled. "And she adores your little boy."

"What if she fires me?"

"This is going to come out one way or another," Vivano pointed out. "She *will* find out about your involvement with Ivan, unless you plan to keep it a secret forever. "Wouldn't you rather she find out *before* they arrest Ivan's father?"

"So basically, I have to choose between being fired tomorrow or being fired later in the week."

"I doubt you'll be fired," Laura said. "You still did all the work. You still solved the case, and you did so without divulging confidential information."

He thought of the video, the first one that seemed to clear David Ramsey. He'd certainly shared that information with Ivan. But the smoking gun, the evidence he'd uncovered to crack the case, Ivan knew nothing about.

"And what do I do about Ivan."

"Wait until the arrest is made, and then immediately call him. Be there for him, and accept his reaction, whatever it is." Laura took hold of her boyfriend's hand. "Honesty and openness are the only things that are going to get you through this."

"I should call him right now."

"No!" His three guests said in unison.

"If you do that, you *really* might lose your job," Vivano said. "You'd have to tell him about the arrest. You'd have to give up confidential information. You can't do that, bro. What if he freaks and tips off his dad? What if the man flees the country?"

"Ivan wouldn't do that."

"Even if he doesn't, it's going to mean you'll have to lie to Bri. You'll have to tell her that you haven't told Ivan anything."

Tucker thought about the advice of his coworkers after they left. He tossed and turned, unsure what he was going to do, and unfortunately, the morning light didn't make things any clearer for him. But he knew in his heart they were right. He knew he couldn't be the one to arrest Ivan's dad, and he couldn't compromise the case by notifying Ivan of the arrest before it happened. He had to talk to his boss and come clean about everything. He had to ask for recusal.

~ ~ ~ ~ ~

"So you've been seeing this Ramsey boy all along?" Bri stood in front of her desk, arms folded across her chest.

"Well, he's a man, and no, I haven't been 'seeing' him." Tucker raised his hands, making air quotes. He quickly lowered them when Bri's scowl registered. "Sorry, I mean we actually met before, at the hospital. He was Jaydin's nurse when he had his tonsillectomy."

She shook her head, the most disgusted look on her face. "And you didn't report this to me then, that you knew one of the family members of the victim."

"I...uh...It kind of happened at the same time. The fire occurred early that morning, and I met Ivan right after I left the scene of the crime. I didn't know there was any connection..."

She held up her hand to silence him. "In other words, even after you did connect the dots and figured out that Ivan Ramsey was the victim's son, you did not report this to me, you did not ask for reassignment."

"I'm sorry. I thought about it. I went back and forth, knowing there was the potential for a conflict of interest."

"There's more than fucking potential here, Brown! What the fuck were you thinking?"

"But I honestly didn't compromise the case. I didn't tell Ivan about any of this evidence that we've gathered against his father."

She closed her eyes a second, sighing, and shook her head. When she opened them, she stepped around the desk and took her seat in the big, comfortable chair. "You leave me no choice, Tucker. I'm sorry, but I have to suspend you." She opened her laptop as he sat there on pins and needles.

"I understand—"

"Quiet!"

She continued typing, staring intently at the screen, and then finally stopped and looked up. She pushed back her chair and stood, then walked over to her printer. She removed the document and handed it to Tucker. "This is your reprimand. Read and sign. Check your weapon and badge before you leave. Report back to work at the end of your suspension."

He looked down at the paper. "Two days? Really?"

"Tucker, I reviewed everything in the case. It's solid. You did your legwork, and I don't think there is going to be any issue with convicting this motherfucker. And *that* is the only thing that saved you. Letting yourself become romantically involved with a person of interest in a criminal investigation you're working on is stupid! You're smart enough. I don't even need to waste my breath with this lecture."

He nodded and looked down. "Thank you. Thank you for not…"

"Oh, don't thank me. Don't you dare, because not only are you suspended for two days, but when you come back you're on probation for another ninety."

He looked up, panicked. "Does that mean…?"

"No, it doesn't mean you can't see your boyfriend. It means you better tow the fucking line. Now get the hell out of my office. Have Viviano call you when he makes the arrest, but do not even think about contacting Ivan until after you receive that call. Then get your ass over to be with him, wherever he is. That poor guy will have lost *both* his parents because of this."

Tucker nodded as he blinked back the sting of tears. "I know." He smiled wanly as he rose from his chair. "Thank you," he mouthed, not daring to speak the words out loud again, and exited his boss's office.

Chapter Twenty

"What the fuck is going on?" Ivan yelled into his phone. "You *lied* to me! You said he didn't do it. You said he was in the clear, his alibi was air tight!"

"I'm sorry." Tucker sounded smaller on the phone, defeated. "I'm here outside the hospital, waiting by your car. Can we please talk?"

"You're waiting by my car? Are you serious? Tucker, I'm working! I'm on my break, and I don't get off for another four hours or so. You had to know about this yesterday. You *had* to. You told me to trust you, said that there'd been a break in the case but you couldn't talk about it. How *could* you? How could you not have warned me?"

He was beginning to lose it. His entire body was trembling as he stood in the employee lounge next to his locker. "Now they're both gone! Both my parents...Tucker...*why*?" He sobbed as he slid to his knees and dropped the phone.

Suddenly arms surrounded him. "Oh God, Ivan are you okay?" It was Carrie.

It all became a blur after that. She led him to another room and had him lie down. Soon a doctor showed up, but Ivan had gone numb. He lay curled in a fetal position, wishing it all had been a horrible dream.

The doctor left, and Ivan wrapped his arms around himself. At last Carrie returned, and he pushed himself up to sit on the side of the bed. She held out her hand to him. "Take this." Without arguing, he removed the pill from her hand and slipped it into his mouth. She held up a small cup of water which he gulped in order to swallow the pill.

He was in the sleeping lounge, the tiny area where hospital staff took naps. Doctors and nurses, when they had to work double or triple shifts often rested here while on their breaks.

"Ivan…" Carrie slid onto the mattress beside him. "I think you had a panic attack…or something. We can admit you…"

"No, he shook his head."

"You can come to my house. I don't think you should be alone. Or I can call your brother."

"Or you can come to my house."

Ivan looked up, and there stood Tucker at the threshold of the door. He took a step toward Ivan.

"They told me at the nurses' station where to find you. Ivan, please, I'm so sorry…"

Ivan looked up into his eyes. He didn't know what to say, think, or feel. "Did he really do it?" Ivan whispered. "Please tell me you're not sure."

Tucker sighed, and in that moment Ivan could see the sympathy and love in his eyes. "I'm sorry, Ivan, but yes. I think he did do it. I'm sure of it, and God only knows how much I wanted to tell you. I even came close to telling you, but I couldn't. Not only would it have compromised the case — which…" he waved his hand in a dismissive gesture… "*Fuck* the case! I don't care about the case. I care about *you*. Ivan, how could I have put you in that position? If I'd have told you, you'd have had to make a choice whether to help your father or remain silent for my sake."

He continued to gaze into Tucker's eyes. "Not just for your sake. For Mom's sake, too."

Tucker nodded. He seemed afraid to come any closer.

Carrie stood up. "He's traumatized right now. This might not be such a good idea…"

"No," Ivan said. "He's fine. We need to talk."

She reached over to rub Ivan's back. "We got someone to cover the rest of your shift...tomorrow too."

"I'll take him home," Tucker said.

She looked at Ivan, apparently waiting for his approval. Ivan nodded. "It's okay, he said again."

When she stepped out of the room, Tucker moved in to take her place on the mattress. He sat next to Ivan and wrapped his arm around him, pulling him against his chest. "I didn't want it to be your dad. I didn't want you to have to go through any more than you have already."

"I can't believe what a monster he's become. How could he do something like this? He could have just fucking divorced her."

"People do horrible things for money. By killing your mother and burning down the house, he was due to receive the insurance on both — her *and* the house."

"He took our mother from us forever. And he even killed our family dog in the process. The house we grew up in — gone. It all just feels like a nightmare that never ends."

"I want to be here for you, Ivan. I can't pretend to understand the hurt that you feel, but I want to be by your side through every minute of it."

Ivan turned to him, staring directly into his eyes. "Why?" he whispered.

"Because I love you."

And they kissed.

~ ~ ~ ~ ~

Tucker spoke with the doctor who had looked in on Ivan at the hospital before Tucker took Ivan home. She didn't believe that he was exhibiting any symptoms that indicated a physical problem. They could admit him and run costly tests, but under the circumstances, she felt his anxiety attack was brought on by stress and grief. She prescribed a sedative and suggested he see a mental health professional.

Tucker was no doctor, but he agreed at least with the last part of her assessment. Poor Ivan had been through so much, and he could probably use some guidance in coping with the harrowing circumstances of his mother's murder at the hands of his own father. Shit, Tucker could use the guidance himself. He honestly didn't know the right thing to do or say.

He was a cop, for fuck's sake. The culture of his profession informed him that when facing tough situations, you just pulled yourself up by the bootstraps and fucking dealt with it. If only life were that simple…

He took Ivan home with him, and by the time he arrived at the house, Ivan was sound asleep in the passenger seat of the car. Tucker didn't bother waking him, but managed to scoop him up into his arms and carry him like a groom carrying his bride over a threshold. He marched all the way down the hall, carrying Ivan in his arms, and gently deposited him on his bed where he covered him with a light blanket. He turned the fan on low to keep him cool and headed back to the living room to make some calls.

Sitting on the sofa, he picked up the remote and turned on the TV. He checked the local news, and sure enough, they already were covering the arrest in depth. They'd obtained a mugshot of David Ramsey and somehow had found out about the insurance money. Their story portrayed him as an upstanding member of his church, a deacon, who was also a successful businessman and father of two but had somehow gone wrong. They recounted the grizzly details of the homicide and arson, and as Tucker watched, he was relieved that Ivan wasn't awake to see it.

In the weeks to come, the media could exploit Ivan's relationship with Tucker. He could only imagine the headline: Gay Cop Caught in Affair with Son of Murderer/Arsonist He Convicted. Why did they always have to do that? Anything "gay" was susceptible to sensationalism or scandal. He and Ivan were going to have to decide going forward how open they were willing to be about their relationship.

Well, he didn't even know if Ivan *wanted* a relationship, and Tucker wasn't about to pressure him at this stage. Ivan needed support, love, and however much time was necessary for him to heal. The case, though cracked, was far from over. Even if David Ramsey cooperated and confessed to the murder, the process of arraignment, sentencing, and so forth could take months. If he were to fight it and plead not guilty, there would be a trial, and that could take a year or more.

Tucker picked up the phone. The first calls he made were the easiest. He called Viviano to make sure everything was okay. They talked about how the arrest went down, how Ramsey acted flabbergasted, said he was innocent. They made the arrest at Diane Seaver's home which was where he was staying since he returned from Florida. Boy, that was going to give the press a field day once they started digging into that piece of the story.

"Thanks for the advice last night," Tucker said. "Man, you guys talked some sense into me, somehow got through my thick skull."

"Yeah, well it wasn't easy." Viviano laughed. "You're right, it's pretty fucking thick."

He then called Janelle who happened to have just watched the news coverage. "I was going to call you but I didn't know if I should wait. How is Ivan?"

"He lost it, Janelle. He pretty much freaked, had a meltdown at the hospital. They gave him a sedative, and I brought him back here. He's sleeping on my bed."

"Oh my God, poor thing."

"Mommy, Mommy, is Ivan sick?" Tucker could hear his little boy in the background.

"Yes honey, but he's going to be okay. Daddy's taking care of him."

Tucker then bit the bullet and called Ivan's brother. That was the call he dreaded the most, but to his surprise, Brandon was pretty decent. "Man, why'd you lie to my brother? Why couldn't you be straight with him...well, I mean... not 'straight' as in... Oh dude, fuck. What am I saying? Why couldn't you just be fucking honest?"

"I never lied to him, but there were things about the investigation I wasn't allowed to discuss."

"Can I talk to him?"

"I'll have him call you when he wakes up. He pretty much broke down at the hospital. They had to give him a sedative, and he's still sleeping."

"At the hospital!"

"No, he's fine. He's with me at my house."

Brandon did not immediately respond. "Well I appreciate you looking out for my baby bro. Man, you better not do him wrong. Cop or no cop, you don't fuck with my brother."

"I hear you, and I promise, I will never hurt him on purpose."

"Or on accident!"

Tucker smiled. "And hopefully not on accident."

"I knew Dad did. I knew almost from the fucking beginning. I just could sense by the way he acted at the funeral, the way he responded to family during the visitation. Something wasn't right, and when I was able to pull his credit card statements…"

"How did you do that, anyway?"

"He had to use my laptop. His burned up in the fire."

"He didn't have it with him on his 'business trip'."

Brandon laughed. "Yeah, right. Business trip to Deckerville. Why would you need to get a motel when you're only two hours from home? No, he said he'd forgotten to take it with him on that trip. Might be true, but then again I think the only business he planned to do was between the sheets with his girlfriend. And it also might have contained shit he needed to get rid of. Hey, wait, should I be telling you all this?"

"Doesn't matter now, I'm not on the case. Might have been nice if you'd told me all of it before, although I discovered most of it on my own."

Brandon sighed. "I know, man. It's hard, though. I want justice for our mom, but like Ivan said, he's the only parent we have left. Hard to wrap your mind around that."

"I'd like to have you and your girlfriend over sometime, maybe for a cookout or something. Just the four of us."

"That'd be cool, or we're down with you coming here. Either way."

"Thanks for being such an awesome big bro to Ivan."

"You ain't gotta thank me for that."

~ ~ ~ ~ ~

Ivan awoke to darkness and didn't at first know where he was. As his eyes adjusted, he realized he was at Tucker's, in his bed. He had no memory of how he got there. He rose from the bed and rubbed his face. He remembered leaving the hospital with Tucker and riding in his car, but after that…nothing.

God, he was thirsty enough to drain a camel. He crept out of the bedroom and padded down the hall to the bathroom where he washed his face and rinsed his dry mouth with tap water. After using the bathroom, he headed out to the kitchen where he found Tucker.

"Something smells good."

Tucker looked up from the stove. "How you feeling?" He set down the wooden spoon he was holding and walked over to Ivan, embracing him.

"It's so weird. I feel like a jellyfish, like the muscles in my body relaxed so much that my bones turned to mush."

"That's what those valiums do. They relax you, help you sleep."

Ivan walked over to the fridge and got himself a bottled water or which he drank about half in one swig. "I'm sorry about—"

"Don't be. Babe, you have nothing to apologize for. I'm the one who's sorry. I wish I could have told you this weekend what was happening."

"And ruin our perfect weekend? Nah, you did it the right way. I'm glad I didn't know." He took another sip, this time of an average amount.

"Really?" Tucker walked over to him and took Ivan's face in his hands as he stared into his eyes.

"Really."

"I don't know how to cook many things. Spaghetti's one of them, so that's what we're having."

"I'm starving, but what time is it?"

"A little after eleven."

"Eleven o'clock at night, and you're cooking spaghetti." He smiled, then laughed. "That's crazy."

"Figured you'd be hungry."

"Now that I know the truth about what happened to Mom, a lot of the puzzle pieces have fallen into place. Dad's weird behavior. The diamond ring. The business trips. There were a lot of unexplained things, loose ends, that were hard to understand."

"Yeah." Tucker stepped back over to the stove, adjusting the burner heat as he stirred.

"And you know what? I'm pissed more than ever by the things he said to me Saturday morning. When he said he had called Mom, I wonder if he actually had. I doubt it. I bet she told him about my conversation with her before she died…when he showed up to kill her."

"It's possible."

"I wonder if she said anything else to him. I wonder if one of the last things she said before she died was that her son was gay."

"And that she loved him just the way he is."

"I think I'm going to just pretend that's exactly what happened." Ivan smiled. "I'm not even going to confront him and ask him. I'm going to assume it to be true. Mom had accepted me, and she wanted Dad to as well."

"I think you're probably right."

"Give me a taste." He pointed to the sauce. Tucker scooped a tiny bit onto the wooden spoon, then blew on it. He stepped back over to Ivan, holding one hand under the spoon as he positioned it in front of Ivan's mouth.

"Mm. Good. Did you add oregano? Basil?"

"It's from a jar." Tucker laughed, probably louder than he should have, and Ivan joined in.

"Well, it's fucking perfect! You're a chef!"

~ ~ ~ ~ ~

At one in the morning they were spooned together in the bathtub, Ivan in front of Tucker. Tucker wrapped his soapy arms around Ivan's slippery chest.

"Good thing you have one of these huge garden tubs. You need it with your long legs."

It felt so wonderful to Tucker to have this man in his arms. "You're not that much shorter than me."

"A good half a foot, at least. I'm six-foot-one."

"Yeah, exactly six inches. That's still a decent height. I think we fit perfectly together."

"Mm, more or less. You do have to bend your knees a bit when I fuck you from behind."

Tucker laughed. "Don't get me excited in the bathtub. I might accidentally stab you with something."

"Your weapon?" Ivan slid his hand underwater, and Tucker moaned as he felt Ivan's fingers slide around his shaft.

"I had to turn in my weapon at the precinct. And my badge."

Ivan released his grip and turned to face Tucker. "What? Why?"

"It's just for two days. I got suspended."

"Oh my God, please tell me it wasn't because of me."

"It was just for *two days*. It's no big deal, and no, it wasn't because of you. It's because of a decision *I* made. I should have recused myself from the case a lot sooner, as soon as I became interested in you. Which was, well, kind of right at the beginning."

"That's horrible! I don't think that's right."

"I could have been suspended a lot longer, or demoted. I could have even been fired. I'm thankful I only got a couple days. Basically it's like a warning."

"I think I know what might make the suspension worth it. Sit up here." Ivan tapped against the side of the tub, an area where you someone could sit while soaking their feet.

Tucker grinned. "What are you up to?"

"Just do it."

Tucker pushed himself out of the water and sat on the edge of the tub. Ivan moved over between his legs and spread them apart, staring up at Tucker's face. He then looked down at Tucker's raging hardon, leaned forward, and devoured it in one gulp.

"Ahh, shit! You're right…totally fucking worth it."

Chapter Twenty-One

Ivan sat in the cubicle, waiting, and when his father entered the adjacent room and walked up to chair on the other side of the partition, they did not immediately make eye contact. Once he sat down, they were staring face to face. Ivan had witnessed this scene more time than he could remember on television and in movies, but this was the first time he'd ever actually visited someone in jail. Unlike some of the movies, there were no phones. They merely spoke to each other over the partition.

"Ivan," his father said.

"Your trial starts tomorrow."

He nodded, offering no commentary.

"Well…I just thought I'd come see you. I haven't talked to you since…"

"They arrested me four months ago. I know. Neither has your brother."

Ivan clenched his jaw. "I wouldn't count on him paying you a visit. He may *never* be able to do that. He's been very hurt by this…I mean, by what you've done."

"By what *I've* done?"

Could it really be possible that Ivan's father didn't have a clue as to how he had devastated Brandon and him? Could he not comprehend the moral bankruptcy of his actions? He'd committed murder, for God's sake. Many children, regardless their age, might never be able to forgive a parent for that, but in this case, Ivan's father hadn't just killed a stranger on the street. He'd killed Ivan's own mother.

"Yeah." Ivan glared at him. "By what *you've* done. You know, shooting our mother, burning up her body, torching the home we grew up in—and with Rocket in it!" She was their collie. "Those things hurt. They hurt a *lot*."

"I haven't been convicted of anything."

"Christ, Dad!" Ivan leaned back, distancing himself from the glass—and his father. "Your attorney is arguing a defense of temporary insanity. You're not even fucking denying you did it!"

"But it's true. Your mother…" A very dark, angry expression washed over the man's demeanor. He didn't even resemble Ivan's father, and it was kind of creepy. "She got what she asked for. She was a miserable, hateful woman, Ivan. And she wanted to make all the rest of us miserable right along with her."

"What are you fucking talking about?"

"She was furious when she found out about Diane and me. She was going to divorce me, take at least half of everything."

"She fucking deserved at least half of everything. She was married to you for over thirty years."

"She'd have left me bankrupt. She'd have destroyed our only chance at happiness. I don't think God would have wanted that. He wouldn't have expected us to go the rest of our lives barely scraping by, not after we'd worked so hard to acquire what we had."

Ivan couldn't stop shaking his head. He sat there with his mouth agape, dumbfounded by what he was hearing. "Dad, you know what? Your attorney's probably right. You *are* insane. In any event, there's another reason why I'm here. Not that it means a damn thing to you, but I'll tell you nonetheless. I've fallen in love with someone, and it's gotten very serious. Tucker, the detective who investigated your case…the man responsible for your pending conviction…he is my boyfriend. No wait, I misspoke. He is my *fiancé*." Ivan held up his left hand to display the ring he'd received the night before. "It's going to be a December wedding. Holiday themed. Unfortunately, I'm sure you probably won't make it. We'll send an invitation anyway…to the penitentiary."

"You're sick." His father glared. "An abomination." He slid his chair back, pushing himself away from the counter.

"See you tomorrow, Dad. Good luck in court."

~ ~ ~ ~ ~

The trial lasted longer than Ivan expected. He'd taken a week's vacation in order to attend, but it was going to extend into the following week. He'd made arrangements with work to be off the duration, even if he had to use personal days to cover his absence.

He really did love Tucker. He'd fallen hard, head over heels, and with each passing day, his love grew stronger. He really didn't know it was possible to feel so connected to another person. He smiled when he thought about how annoying Tucker had seemed when he first met him. Now all those things that once had irked him were the characteristics Ivan cherished most.

Yeah, he was a stubborn as a mule. And he didn't have the best manners, didn't know a thing about etiquette. He'd probably never become a gourmet cook or anything close. He had no clue how to select a decent wine or even fold a fitted sheet.

But he could barbecue up a storm. He could make some mean Mickey-Mouse pancakes. He gave the best back massages, and when he was drinking, his two-note-flat Karaoke melted Ivan's heart. And most importantly, he was an awesome daddy. God, was he wonderful with Jaydin. There wasn't a doubt in Ivan's mind he'd made the right decision when he accepted Tucker's proposal.

On the last day of the trial, Tucker came with Ivan to listen to the closing arguments. When the judge adjourned for jury deliberation, Ivan heaved a sigh of relief that this part was over. He'd cried through much of the prosecution's closing presentation. They'd described in detail how David Ramsey had planned and executed his plan, how he'd murdered his wife in cold blood and then set the house on fire.

His mom was gone forever, and Ivan would never know for sure exactly where his relationship with her would have ended up had she lived. They'd always been so close that Ivan had to cling to the belief she would have come around. He knew it in his heart, that she'd already decided before she died to accept him for who he was.

He and Tucker left the courtroom and walked down town to find a place to get a bite to eat. Ivan would receive a text if the jury was ready to announce a verdict. He didn't expect it to be a long deliberation, but he at least thought it would be long enough for him to eat a sandwich. He was wrong. Twenty-eight minutes after the jury went out, they delivered their verdict.

Tucker and Ivan, along with several dozen others, hurriedly headed back to the courtroom.

"Madame Foreman, have you reached a verdict in the case of the State of Ohio versus David Andrew Ramsey."

"We have your honor." She handed the printed verdict to the bailiff who delivered it to the judge. He looked at it and refolded the paper, his facial expression completely blank. He handed it back to the bailiff.

"You may read the verdict please."

"In the matter before the court of the State of Ohio versus defendant, David Andrew Ramsey, on the count of murder in the first degree, the jury hereby finds the defendant *guilty*."

Gasps and sighs of relief erupted in the courtroom. The judge held up a hand for silence. Ivan looked over at his father who stood like a statue.

"In the matter before the court of the State of Ohio versus defendant, Dadid Andre wRamsey, on the count of first-degree criminal arson, the jury hereby finds the defendant *guilty.*"

The went through the long list of charges against Ivan's father, and on every count, they found him guilty. Ivan wondered how they'd even had time to go through the list in the brief, twenty-eight minute time period. But there was little doubt that his father had done it, that he'd planned it and was of sound mind when he carried out his actions.

Surprisingly, Ivan didn't devolve into a fit of tears. He didn't feel devastated by the verdict, nor did he feel overjoyed. He was thankful for justice, but really, there could never be *true* justice. He'd never have his mother back. He'd never have an opportunity to build a future together, to make her a part of his life with Tucker and Jaydin.

That was the aspect that made Ivan sad. His mom was going to miss the chance to be a grandma to his adorable little boy.

Tucker and Ivan walked out of the courtroom hand-in-hand. Ivan couldn't care less if a reporter noticed or made something of it. They both were now a hundred percent out in their jobs and now in the community.

"I want to do something in Mom's memory," Ivan said.

"What did you have in mind?" They had stopped just outside the courthouse.

"I don't know yet, maybe make a donation of some sort, start are scholarship fund in her name? I've got to give it some though."

And at that moment an unfamiliar face approached. "Excuse me, are you Ivan Ramsey?" Ivan hesitated, thinking perhaps the young man was a reporter. Tucker stepped between Ivan and the twentysomething blond.

"Who wants to know?"

"Um, I'm Sherman Richards, and I work with the LGBT homeless youth program in Dayton. We have a branch in Deckerville, sadly. I mean, it's sad there would even be a need for one there, but ya know, this *is* the Bible Belt."

"W-wait." Ivan stopped him. "What is it you all do?"

"We have shelters for homeless teens and young adults who've been kicked out of their homes and churches for being LGBT."

"Oh my God," Ivan said, holding a hand over his heart.

"Anyway, I just wanted to thank you...or actually to thank your mother, but since she is sadly no longer with us, to thank *you* on her behalf. She made a very large contribution to our organization in your name."

"Wh-what? Wait, are you sure?"

"Oh, I'm positive. And the truly amazing thing is that we received the check after her untimely passing. It was dated the day before she died."

Ivan held both hands to his face and began to weep. Tucker held hem, wrapping him in a warm embrace.

"Thank you! Thank you so much!"

Ivan gently pulled away from Ivan and pulled Sherman into a fierce hug. "And we will be making another donation very soon...in my mother's name, this time."

Chapter Twenty-Two

Ivan waited nervously in the shadows, listening for the opening strains of the song Tucker had selected for their processional march. Though Ivan argued for Bruno Mars, Tucker's choice of an Elton John classic won out. As usual, he was right. The Bruno Mars' song was more upbeat, and they'd save that for the recessional as they were walking away from the altar, already married.

He hadn't been allowed to see his groom yet, which was why the song, "Something About the Way You Look Tonight" seemed all the more appropriate. They'd see each other dressed in their tuxedos for the first time at the altar, and that's where they'd exchange their personal vows they each had written for the other.

Ivan smiled as he remembered the way he'd at first misjudged Tucker. He'd seen him as arrogant and smug, then later learned he was exactly the opposite. He'd assumed Tucker to be a pretentious man on a power trip, hiding from his own identity, but Tucker proved to be the most honest, straightforward person Ivan had ever known.

As the music started, Ivan stared straight ahead and began moving slowly down the aisle. Their guests immediately rose from their seats, some turning to look in Ivan's direction while others choosing to watch Tucker. Ivan refused to glance over, though. He looked straight down the aisle and continued until he reached the very end. At that point he then turned and looked up, staring across the stage at a pair of deep brown eyes looking directly back at him.

Ivan's heart leapt within his chest.

Now with their eyes locked on each other, they moved closer together, and the sight of this stunning man nearly stole Ivan's breath. They stopped as they approached each other, and Ivan extended his arms, just as they'd rehearsed. Tucker slipped his hands into Ivan's and they gazed into each other's eyes.

"Friends and family, we're gathered together on this most joyous occasion," began Briana Nguyen. They'd chosen Tucker's boss to officiate. "To join in matrimony this couple, Ivan Ramsey and Tucker Brown."

Standing alongside Ivan was the only person he'd even considered as a best man, his brother Brandon. Tucker had chosen his partner, Viviano.

"The couple has chosen to exchange vows they've written themselves. We'll begin with Ivan."

Ivan took a deep breath and looked up into Tucker's face.

"Why is it that I'm marrying a cop?" he began, and his question was met with soft laughter from their guests. "I know I didn't plan this. I didn't set out for this to happen. It just did. One minute I was yelling at you, calling you all kinds of names and accusing you of being a pretentious jerk, and the next minute you had me in your arms kissing me.

"I was never looking for a savior. I didn't ask for a hero. Of course, you are both of these things to me, but that's not why I'm madly in love with you. I don't want someone who can save me from the perils and hardships of life, who can rescue me from my own self-loathing. I want a man who'll be there with me when times are good, and when times are bad, walking hand-in-hand with me through this journey.

"You've helped complete me, Tucker Brown. You've helped make me a better man, and I love you and Jaydin with all my heart. And for these reasons I want to share the rest of my life with you."

At this point, Tucker's parents urged Jaydin forward. He stepped up to the altar, standing in front of the two grooms, and Ivan looked down at him smiling. He removed one of the rings that had been pinned to velvet pillow Jaydin was holding and slipped it on Tucker's finger.

"Tucker, please share your vows." Bri smiled warmly.

"Ivan..." He stopped and took a breath, obviously nervous. "I'm not used to talking in front of so many people." He continued to stare into Ivan's eyes. "I love you so much. You're so smart and sexy and have the biggest heart on the planet. And you're amazing with Jaydin. He loves you too, with all his heart. Don't ya, Jay?"

"Yes!"

Ivan smiled, blinking back tears.

"I denied for a real long time who I really am, and it took the love and patience of some wonderful people to get me out of my shell — my *closet*. At one point, I felt like it was best that I just give up. I didn't know how to do this thing, how to be this person that I am. But then you came along, and suddenly all the pieces started to fit. You were everything I'd ever been looking for, and I knew then and there that if there really was such a thing as a soul mate, you were it. You are the real deal, and I couldn't love you any more than I do. Well, that's what I say now, but I'm guessing if you asked me tomorrow, I'd say I love you even more."

He sighed and shook his head. "I've gone and rattled on, forgot everything I memorized. I'm sorry. I'll let you read it later. It was a pretty nice little speech." Laughter erupted. "What I want you to know now...and all these good people here...is that I love you with all my heart and want you to be my husband."

He turned and took the ring from Jaydin's pillow, then slipped it onto Ivan's finger.

Tucker's mom motioned Jaydin back to his seat, and Bri smiled once more. "Damn you Tucker." She reached up to wipe away a tear. "I'm gonna have to put you on probation again. Made me cry."

Laughter filled the chapel, but only briefly, because the seriousness of the occasion quickly settled in.

"Tucker Brown, do you take this man, Ivan Ramsey, to be your lawful husband, to love and to cherish, in sickness and health, from this day forward until the rest of your life?"

"I do." He smiled broadly.

"Ivan Ramsey, do you take this man , Tucker Brown, to be *your* lawful husband, to love and to cherish, in sickness and health, from this day forward for the rest of your life?"

"I do." The tears began to flow.

"By the power vested in my by the Supreme Court of the United States of America, I now pronounce you legally married! You may now kiss!"

Tucker grabbed hold of him, passionately delivering a powerful kiss as the cheers erupted around them.

When they pulled apart, Ivan smiled broadly and grabbed hold of his husband's hand. Together they looked out on the congregation, raising their connected hands into the air. The music began, "Just the Way You Are" by Bruno Mars, and they marched briskly down the aisle into their future together…

…where they lived happily ever after.

About the Author:

Jeff Erno began writing in the early 1990s. Originally his work was posted on a free, amateur website, where it was eventually discovered and published. He writes gay-themed stories that span several subgenres including young adult, m/m romance, gay fiction, BDSM, and sci-fi.Until recently, Erno worked as a retail store manager but now writes full-time. He currently resides in southern Michigan. He loves animals, particularly cats, and enjoys reading, movies, theater, country-western music, community service, political activism, and cake decorating. Website: www.jefferno.com

More Jeff Erno titles available from Ai Press

Speedy Rewards
Baggage
Forever Young
Forever Fearless
Final Destiny (Kokoro Press imprint)

Whether you prefer e-books or paperbacks, be sure to visit Ai Press on the web at www.ai-press.net for an erotic reading experience that will leave you breathless. In Japanese, "ai" means love. At Ai Press, it means unbridled passion!

www.ai-press.net

Made in the USA
Lexington, KY
24 September 2019